Saint Christopher

Saint Christopher

A NOVELLA

José Maria de Eça de Queirós

foreword by CARLOS REIS

translated from the Portuguese by

GREGORY RABASSA & EARL E. FITZ

TAGUS PRESS
UMass Dartmouth
Dartmouth,
Massachusetts

ADAMASTOR SERIES 9

Tagus Press at UMass Dartmouth

www.portstudies.umassd.edu

© 2015 The University of Massachusetts Dartmouth

All rights reserved

Manufactured in the United States of America

General Editor: Frank F. Sousa / Managing Editor: Mario Pereira

Copyedited by Rosemary Williams

Designed and typeset in Jenson by Eric M. Brooks

For all inquiries, please contact:

Tagus Press at UMass Dartmouth

Center for Portuguese Studies and Culture

285 Old Westport Road / North Dartmouth MA 02747-2300

Tel. 508-999-8255 / Fax 508-999-9272

www.portstudies.umassd.edu

FUNDAÇÃO
LUSO-AMERICANA

*Publication of this book was made possible in part
by a grant from the Luso-American Foundation.*

Library of Congress Cataloging-in-Publication Data

Queirós, Eça de, 1845–1900. author. / [São Cristóvão. English]

Saint Christopher: a novella / José Maria de Eça de Queirós;
foreword by Carlos Reis; translated from the Portuguese by
Gregory Rabassa and Earl E. Fitz.

  pages cm. — (Adamastor series; 9)

ISBN 978-1-933227-62-7 (pbk.: alk. paper) —

ISBN 978-1-933227-63-4 (ebook)

I. Rabassa, Gregory, translator. II. Fitz, Earl E., translator. III. Title.

PQ9261.E3S3613   2015

869.3'3 — dc23   2014037565

5 4 3 2 1

Contents

Foreword

NOTES ON SAINTHOOD
IN EÇA DE QUEIRÓS

Carlos Reis

 Any reader who is unaware of the complexity and diversity of Eça de Queirós's oeuvre or familiar primarily with the long-established mainstream perspective on his writings will likely be surprised by this story. *Saint Christopher* is a hagiography, a life of a saint, that harbors themes and values apparently incompatible with the dominant meanings ascribed to the canonical Eça, stereotyped as his image has been by much literary history. After all, according to this stereotype, the author of *The Crime of Father Amaro* was a fierce critic of Roman Catholicism, the Church, religion, and religious sentiment.

Before I look more closely at this image of Eça in order to discern its various components — those which hold up to scrutiny and those which do not — some initial information about the origin and history of *Saint Christopher* is in order. The novella was published for the first time in 1912, in the volume *Últimas Páginas* (Last Pages), which contained the lives of three saints: Saint Christopher, Saint Onuphrius, and Saint Friar Gil. In addition, several other important texts, unpublished at the time of the author's death in 1900, were also included in the volume: a letter by Carlos Fradique Mendes (left out of *The Correspondence of Fradique Mendes* published in 1900), a letter from Eça to Camilo Castelo Branco, and the essay "O 'Francesismo'" (The "Gallicism"), among others. But the editor, Luís de Magalhães, erred in his choice of the volume's title: these were not yet Eça's *last* pages. The years that followed saw the appearance of a number of unpublished writings that had come close to being lost, including the novels *A Capital!* (The Capital!), *Alves & Ca.* (Alves & Co.), and *O Conde de Abranhos* (Count of Abranhos).

Eça's lives of saints, along with his other posthumous works, present editorial challenges well known to those familiar with the process of their publication: many of the manuscripts that remained unpublished in the course of the author's life are incomplete. At best, they merely had not undergone the final revision, which sometimes led Eça to add to, cut, and otherwise revise his texts when they were already in the form of page proofs, exasperating his editors and typesetters. The ongoing critical edition of the writer's works — with fifteen volumes published to date by Imprensa Nacional-Casa da Moeda — has sought to resolve, whenever possible, precisely such complex editorial problems as have emerged in this scenario. Eça's *Lendas de Santos* (Legends of Saints) — which include *Saint Christopher* — have not been immune from these difficulties, which at the same time fascinate scholars interested in genetic and textual criticism.

To sum up the textual status of the three legends, existing editions of *Saint Christopher* cannot be assessed as to their philological accuracy because Eça's original manuscript has not been preserved. *Santo Onofre* presents substantial problems: although the writing in the manuscript flows relatively smoothly, the evidence of a few significant cuts, additions, and revisions to the wording, in addition to a lack of clarity about the ordering of narrative sequences, mean that the text is nowhere near its prospective definitive form. Until a few years ago, only an outline of *São Frei Gil* was known; the recently uncovered manuscript of this legend is similar, roughly speaking, to that of *Santo Onofre*, although here the story ends abruptly, suggesting the author's intention to continue the narrative.[1] The future critical edition of *Lendas dos Santos* will offer an opportunity to introduce some measure of order into these writings, left unfinished by Eça de Queirós.

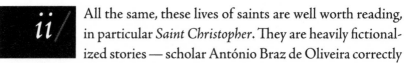 All the same, these lives of saints are well worth reading, in particular *Saint Christopher*. They are heavily fictionalized stories — scholar António Braz de Oliveira correctly dubbed them Eça's "hagiofantasies" — that allow for the articulation of a very interesting dialogue between the *fin-de-siècle* Eça who wrote them

1. See Carlos Reis, "Nótula sobre três manuscritos queirosianos," in *Leituras* 7, series 3, 2001, pp. 131–39.

and the Eça who since the 1870s had seemingly narrowed down his view of religion to a perspective of militant anticlericalism.[2]

By now we have understood that such militancy neither contained nor exhausted the complex, evolving, and ambivalent view of religion, the Catholic Church, and Christianity to be found in Eça's fiction. This view — which, as I have implicitly made clear, encompasses distinct entities and institutions — reflects the positions that Eça assumed and revised with regard to the Christian message, Roman Catholic practices, the interpreters of Catholicism, sainthood, and evangelical solidarity.

To illustrate, let us consider the novel *The Crime of Father Amaro*, recalling that, together with *The Relic*, this was the work that most decisively contributed to Eça de Queirós having been regarded as an "enemy" of the Catholic Church. This enemy status was then projected onto the ground of his recognition as a canonical writer and for a long time made impartial analysis of these (and other) works difficult.

One episode in *The Crime of Father Amaro* allows for a reflection on the topic that interests us in particular here, Eça's understanding of sainthood. It occurs in Chapter 4, during a dinner at which a group of priests yield to the temptations of gluttony, classified by the Church doctrine as a cardinal sin. It is then that the reader encounters the following description of the space in which their gathering is taking place:

> On the sideboard, amongst various books, a figure of Christ, with yellow skin and scarlet wounds, stood sadly on a pedestal against the wall; and beside him, cheerful saints beneath glass domes recalled the gentler side of religion: the kindly giant St Christopher crossing the river with, on his shoulder, the divine child, smiling and bouncing the world in his hand like a ball; the gentle shepherd St John dressed in the fleece of a sheep and wielding not a crook but a cross; the good gatekeeper St Peter, carrying in his clay hand the two holy keys that open the locks to Heaven! On the walls, in garish lithographs, the patriarch St Joseph was leaning on a crook from which white lilies

2. António Braz de Oliveira, "São Cristóvão, sonho e sentido da Geração de Setenta. Notas para uma releitura da hagiofantasia queirosiana," in *150 Anos com Eça de Queirós. III Encontro Internacional de Queirosianos* (São Paulo: Centro de Estudos Portugueses, Universidade de São Paulo, 1997), pp. 83–112.

bloomed; St George's rearing horse trampled the belly of a startled dragon; and good St Anthony was standing by the side of a stream, smiling and talking to a shark. The clink of glasses and the clatter of knives filled the room and its smoke-blackened oak ceiling with unaccustomed jollity.[3]

First of all, we should note here an early appearance of Saint Christopher, visualized according to the terms of traditional hagiographic imagery in the same form in which he will reappear, much later in Eça's work, in the story that bears his name. In addition, however, what I wish to stress about this passage is the following. As he recounts the dinner and describes the priests' behavior, the narrator observes (and makes the reader observe) a discrete space within this scene that harbors images and meanings disregarded by the diners. The Christ that "with yellow skin and scarlet wounds, stood sadly on a pedestal against the wall," sums up well — not least because of the sadness ascribed to him by Eça's personifying rhetoric — the foresaking by the priests of the virtuous qualities the saints represent: goodness, purity, dedication to the Christian message, militant devotion, and so on. This means also that the anticlerical Eça of the 1870s does not disdain those aspects of religious experience to which the saints give witness. Even in its view of the clergy, *The Crime of Father Amaro* makes an exception in stressing the positive and redemptive qualities of one priest, Father Ferrão, whose behavior differs greatly from that of his gluttonous and immoral counterparts. It is Ferrão who tells Amélia, when she accuses João Eduardo of publishing a derogatory article about Leiria's priests, "The lad was writing not against priests, but against the Pharisees!"[4] All this confirms what Eça stated in a letter to Teófilo Braga (dated March 12, 1878): that the critical and reformist realism of the 1870s did not oppose institutions but merely their deficient practices.

Later on, it is possible to cite various examples along the author's literary trajectory that make obvious Eça's interest in themes and figures

3. Eça de Queiroz, *The Crime of Father Amaro: Scenes from the Religious Life*, translated and with an introduction by Margaret Jull Costa (Sawtry, UK: Dedalus, 2002), p. 98.

4. Eça de Queiroz, *The Crime of Father Amaro*, p. 406.

associated with an evangelical Christianity, which he contrasted, as he had done in *The Crime of Father Amaro*, with the decadence of contemporary clergy. Thus, for instance, in *The Relic* he picked up again on the anticlerical critique while also turning to aspects of religious life that had not been present in the earlier novel; let us review what is of interest to the present discussion in this narrative with an exotic and biblical flavor.

In the course of *The Relic*, Teodorico Raposo, a prospective heir to the vast fortune held by his deeply religious aunt, undertakes a trip to the Holy Land — note, in anticipation, the importance travel will also assume in *Saint Christopher* — with the objective of bringing an impressive relic for the aunt, Dona Patrocínio das Neves. Both the journey and Teodorico's plan to soften his aunt's resistance end badly: he is expelled from her home and forced to confront the contradictions of his moral duplicity. Before this outcome, however, Teodorico witnesses — in a dream that occupies the novel's entire third chapter — the last days of Jesus Christ's life in a Jerusalem that is reconstructed with utmost archaeological care. The narrative, focused on Jesus and the mystery of Resurrection — the central event in the foundation of Christianity — is infused with the presence of human experience and affect at the same time as the nascent religion obtains the trappings of a legend. Moreover, the ways in which *The Relic* represents the time and place of Jesus's life reflect Eça's longstanding fascination with that time and place and with their transcendental importance for Western cultural imagination. His reading of Renan surely contributed to this fascination, as did the memory of Eça's travels in Egypt and Palestine in late 1869, which resulted in an apparently unfinished narrative, "A Morte de Jesus" (Death of Jesus).[5]

iii/ As we have seen by now, Eça's relationship with religion, Christianity, and Christian spiritual legacy — which includes the value of sainthood — greatly exceeded his anticlericalism of the 1870s. While the latter was in fact an organic component of a larger project of ideological reform, it is equally true that over the years its expression gradually lost ground, in texts fictional and

5. "A Morte de Jesus" was published in installments in the newspaper *A Revolução de Setembro* in 1870. It is included in the volume *Contos I*, edited by Marie-Hélène Piwnik, of the *Edição Crítica das Obras de Eça de Queirós* (Imprensa Nacional-Casa da Moeda).

nonfictional alike, to Eça's almost idealistic attraction to the Christian message and to the evangelical notion of sainthood.

In particular, the incarnation of the author that we are now used to calling "the last Eça" demonstrates this realignment clearly. I have in mind here a nonexhaustive assembly of texts from the 1890s that in many respects resonate with *Lendas de Santos* and especially with *Saint Christopher*. The chronicle "Um Santo Moderno" (A Modern Saint), published in *Gazeta de Notícias* (Rio de Janeiro) in 1892, on the occasion of Cardinal Henry Edward Manning's death, spells out a very clear message: it is possible to locate manifestations of an *essential sainthood* in the late nineteenth century, whereby the Franciscan model or the example of Saint Anthony of the Desert may emerge in the midst of urban turmoil. The following year, Eça published (also in *Gazeta de Notícias*) two chronicles that reiterate some of the concerns he had raised in connection with the "modern saint."[6] Both allude to the doubts that he and many others were experiencing with regard to the excesses of scientific "religion," the dogmas of positivist thought, and the aims of democracy. Titled "O Bock Ideal" (The Ideal Glass of Bock) and "Positivismo e Idealismo" (Positivism and Idealism), these texts promote, as alternatives to the positivist belief, the spirit of the Gospel, the practice of life inspired by the Gospel, and even the suggestion of a socially engaged Catholicism, although Eça expressed some reservation with regard to the latter movement's mentor, Melchior de Vogüé (1848–1910). It seems incontrovertible, however, that the antinaturalist reaction described in "Positivismo e Idealismo" in conclusion leads the author to the consolatory opportunity to evoke, in an entirely free and uncensored manner, that "incomparable saint" (Eça's words), Saint Francis of Assisi.

Eça is thus headed in the direction of hagiography and the praise of sainthood. And in the process of defining this direction, as he understands it, he makes evident its singularity when the saints he discusses are of the "modern" variety. As he has done with Cardinal Manning, he also does, for other reasons and in a different fashion, with "Saint" Antero, when he contributes to the *In Memoriam* volume for Antero de

6. The texts published by Eça in *Gazeta de Notícias* were gathered in the volume *Textos de Imprensa IV (da Gazeta de Notícias)* edited by Elza Miné e Neuma Cavalcante (Lisbon: Imprensa Nacional-Casa da Moeda, 2002).

Quental published in 1896, five years after the writer's suicide. By the time he comes to write about his friend, Eça has distanced himself from the tragedy of Antero's death and is able to formulate a commemorative and practically essayistic account of the life and exemplary status of this poet and thinker who at one point had been a leader of his generation. This chronological distance explains also the degree of ambivalence detectable in Eça's analysis, ambivalence that does not detract, nevertheless, from the basic substance of the testimony registered in "Um Génio que era um Santo" (A Genius Who Was a Saint): because of his austere life, his exemplary civic activism, the loftiness of his ideals, and the bitter consistency he evinced in holding on to them, Antero de Quental was also a modern saint.[7]

 Scholars who have written about the notion of sainthood in Eça de Queirós — which has not been a very popular topic in the writer's critical bibliography — have almost uniformly stressed a number of points that need to be registered here.[8]

7. See Carlos Reis, "Um bardo dos tempos novos: a imagem queirosiana de Antero," in *Actas do Congresso Internacional Anteriano* (Ponta Delgada: Univ, dos Açores, 1993), pp. 561–72.

8. See especially the following studies: Orlando Grossegesse, "A santidade como problema discursivo. De *A Relíquia* às *Lendas de Santos*," in *Vária Escrita*, 4, 1997, pp. 139–54; Amarilis Tupiassu, *Eça de Queiroz e os Desassossegos da Santidade* (Belém: Ed. da Univ. Federal do Pará), 2001; Aparecida de Fátima Bueno, "O avesso do franciscanismo em Eça de Queirós," in Marli F. Scarpelli e Paulo M. Oliveira, eds., *Os Centenários: Eça, Freyre e Nobre* (Belo Horizonte: FALE/UFMG, 2001), pp. 25–34; Helena C. Buescu, "Santos, lendas, génios e humanos," in *Congresso de Estudos Queirosianos. IV Encontro Internacional de Estudos Queirosianos. Actas* (Coimbra: Almedina/Instituto de Língua e Literatura Portuguesas, 2002), II, pp. 557–68; Jordi Cerdá, "Eça de Queirós recriador de Lendas de Santos. A hagiografia: um velho género para uma nova estética," ibid., II, pp. 557–68; Ofélia Paiva Monteiro, "Variações ecianas em torno da santidade," ibid., I, pp. 43–58; Ângela Varela, "A ascese da escrita queirosiana — do plano terreno à serra de Jacinto e ao céu de Cristóvão," ibid., I, pp. 363–77; Bruno de Cusatis, "A fraternidade universal nas *Lendas de Santos* de Eça de Queiroz," in *Estudos Anterianos*, 9–10, abril-novembro, 2002, pp. 99–113. All these were of course preceded by Jaime Cortesão's seminal study *Eça de Queiroz e a Questão Social* (Lisbon: Imprensa Nacional-Casa da Moeda, 2001), originally published in 1949.

One of the most elaborate — as well as one of the earliest — reflections on this subject was developed by Jaime Cortesão in the 1940s, in articles published in Brazil and Portugal and then gathered in the volume *Eça de Queiroz e a Questão Social* (issued by Seara Nova).[9] It is important to note that at the time Cortesão produced his studies the construct we now refer to as "the last Eça" had not yet acquired the authority it currently holds in Eça de Queirós scholarship, with its emphasis on formal and substantive meanings of Fradique Mendes, the novel *The City and the Mountains* (1901), or the ideological revision of positivism. Similarly, Eça's figures of saints and reflections on sainthood had not yet received much critical attention prior to Cortesão's pioneering effort.

The figure of Saint Christopher forms the axis on which Cortesão's essay turns. The critic uses the saint and the reflection on society that can be extracted from his story to problematize religious faith in terms he relates to Eça's evolving class status but also to other factors. Two of these factors are, firstly, the depressing rhetoric of decadence that according to Eça inflected art in the late nineteenth century, and, secondly, a parallel form of decadence — that of his Portuguese homeland, made manifest in the humiliating episode of the British Ultimatum. In this context, Cortesão stresses the importance of an idealist renewal of philosophy, as well as the extension of the religious sphere to encompass the field of political praxis. Some key figures in this process are Paul Sabatier, the author of a widely read biography of Saint Francis of Assisi, published in 1893, and Pope Leo XIII who — as is well known — infused his pontificate with an interventionist vigor through his valorization of the Church's social responsibility. This is therefore, for Eça and his contemporaries, a time of change. According to Cortesão, the spiritual thaw that provoked this change in Eça began between 1885 and 1888, when Fradique Mendes reappears[10] and when Eça's faith in socialism gradually transforms from a political into a moral imperative, intersect-

9. Cortesão's book was republished twice, in 1970 by Portugália and in 2001 by Imprensa Nacional-Casa da Moeda. In this section I am drawing partially on the preface I contributed to the latter edition.

10. The fictional author Carlos Fradique Mendes made his original appearance in 1869 as a collective creation.

ing with a revival of the most authentic Christian values. Hence the concept of "Christian socialism," understood by Cortesão as a fundamental ideological direction in late Eça de Queirós; as the essayist states, "Eça . . . saw in Franciscan sainthood the sublimation of socialism and transformed a national tradition into a cosmopolitan vision of the future."[11]

The genesis and writing of *Saint Christopher* (which, according to Cortesão, happened between 1894 and 1897) form an integral and central component of Eça's social vision. Accordingly, the spiritual message conveyed by the saint and his Franciscan attitudes have little to do with the tradition of sterile and antisocial asceticism. Instead, a new kind of mysticism emerges as an active alternative to the traditional askesis: rooted in Christian qualities and the example of Jesus, this brand of Franciscanism allows for a transition from Christ to nature and for an evangelical message composed of pragmatism, tolerance, and self-denial, echoing Tolstoy and anticipating the thought and actions of Gandhi. It can be said to conjugate the religious ideal with a civil conception of sainthood.

The renewal of the field of Eça de Queirós studies in recent decades has encouraged, however, new lines of inquiry into the figures of Eça's saints and, in particular, Saint Christopher. One of these lines was explored by Orlando Grossegesse in an article that analyzes sainthood as a discursive problem, formulated in the context of Eça's postnaturalist drift in the writings I discussed earlier. What Grossegesse views as a recarnivalization of Eça's writing leads him to relate Franciscan sainthood to parody as he reflects on "the fusion of laughter, sainthood, animality and nature as a desirable alternative to the contemporary decline of laughter." As a culminating point of this process, "*Lendas de Santos* and similar texts constitute . . . an attempt to found a 'new writing' capable of confronting dilettantism and pessimism, a language of a 'simple soul' that refuses any form of dogmatism and that educates toward an imperfect worldview driven by laughter."[12] For her part, Ofélia Paiva Mon-

11. Jaime Cortesão, *Eça de Queiroz e a Questão Social* (Lisbon: Imprensa Nacional-Casa da Moeda, 2001), p. 75.

12. Orlando Grossegesse, "A santidade como problema discursivo. De *A Relíquia* às *Lendas de Santos*," above, n. 8., pp. 148–51.

teiro locates the roots of Eça's notion of sainthood in much earlier texts (specifically, in "A Morte de Jesus") and traces a trajectory that emphasizes Eça's attitude of intellectual perplexity toward Jesus, as well as the latter's humanization, staged in *The Relic*. Saint Christopher, a saint "of such polygonal exemplariness," becomes, in a way, one of the terminal points of this trajectory: "he *is born* a saint and remains a saint until his death because, in his radical innocence, he is preserved from evil by the closeness that unites his gigantic and misshapen self to nature." In the final analysis, what Eça's saints attest for Monteiro is the writer's singular (and also divided) relationship with the Church and Christianity: "Although the novelist was definitely not a son of the Church — particularly of the Roman Catholic Church — he nevertheless was, in my reading, a Christian heart fascinated by Jesus, who, like Antero, dreamed of one day coming to rest in God's right hand."[13]

V The story told in *Saint Christopher* unfolds in a medieval time and space. Eça de Queirós expressed clearly and on multiple occasions his fascination with the Middle Ages, although this expression may have been tempered by a guilty conscience. In the cultural context that harbored the ideological and literary project of critical realism, an attraction to history, and particularly medieval history, would have appeared as a concession to the tradition of Romantic medievalism, which in the early 1870s the realist doctrinaire Eça actively contested. But his fascination was impossible to disguise: witness, for example, his 1885 letter to the Count of Ficalho, in which Eça confesses his "latent and guilty appetite for the historical novel." Additional evidence is supplied by the writer's working notes held in his archive in the National Library of Portugal, which demonstrate how methodical Eça was in his labor of gathering information, technical, historical, and ethnographic alike, that was then channeled into works such as — in addition to *Saint Christopher* — the short story "The Hanged Man" and, especially, the novel *The Illustrious House of Ramires*.

What we see described in the hagiographic narrative of *Saint Christo-*

13. Ofélia Paiva Monteiro, "Variações ecianas em torno da santidade," above, n. 8., pp. 54–58.

pher is a world of rough and sometimes brutal custom; social inequality and oppression of the weak; Satanist practices and devout pleas to the Lord; armed conflicts and violent pillage. But besides all this we witness as well values and attitudes of loyalty, courage, hierarchic order, and finally, social rebellion. The protagonist's trajectory is drawn as a long journey from birth to old age; the latter is marked by salvation, through the intervention of a child that is none other than "Jesus Christ, Our Lord and Savior, as small as when he'd been born in the manger and who now, sweetly, kindly, and through the clear, bright morning light, was bearing him up to Heaven." Before this redemptive encounter, Christopher traverses his brutal and unequal world, always putting himself at the service of the weak and the oppressed, and multiplying gestures of humility that seem to contradict his gigantic stature and the physical power his body projects. That is also how Christopher's agency keeps bringing him ever closer to a sainthood achievable in the earthly domain, as he accumulates actions of benevolent surrender to another along with experiences of disillusion brought about by much that he observes and faces: cruelty, ingratitude, egoism, tyranny, and so on.

The sainthood exemplified by Christopher is thus not merely of a contemplative nature: he is a saint shaped by his devotion to the cause of the weakest, as demonstrated in the episode of the Jacquerie, the fourteenth-century peasant revolt against feudal authority and widespread poverty, which was especially harsh in France in the immediate aftermath of the Black Death pandemic.[14] Joining the Jacques, Christopher has no qualms about resorting to violence in a battle in which his comrades are decimated. In the story, their movement seems to stand for a reaction to God's silence or strange absence from an unjust world. Theirs is a God who appears alienated from the society of men and leaves up to the rebels the search for justice that is slow in coming. "And who knows?," asks a mendicant friar; "Incomprehensible are the ways of Providence! Perhaps, to punish the castles, God might raise up in revolt an army from out of the hovels." Finally, the rebellion also seems to spell out an answer to another question, formulated by Chris-

14. The name Jacquerie originated in the derogatory epithet Jacques Bonhomme, a generic designation used to refer to poor peasants who were denied any measure of social dignity.

topher himself: "Why could there not be the same hearth for everyone, the same bread?"

A saint on earth before ascending to Heaven, Eça's Christopher represents, ultimately, a coherent culmination of another passage — that of the writer himself, guided by values from which he had never abstained. And although Eça de Queirós left his *Saint Christopher* unpublished, the story contains a great deal of the passion for social justice and human solidarity that he nearly always inscribed on the horizon of his literary labors.

Translated by Anna M. Klobucka

Saint Christopher

i/ As dusk was falling one day in a forest where the sound of the swineherds' horns was echoing beneath the high tops of the oak trees where the crows were answering with their caws, a woodcutter, a serf in a ragged woolen cloak who had been hard at work ever since the first song of the larks, tucked his hatchet into his leather belt and, along with his mare all loaded down with firewood, went on his way through the village pathways that led to his master's castle.

At each cross nailed to the tree trunks in the forest he would doff his cap of rabbit pelt and say an Ave Maria. As he went along by the lake where the evening sky was at its brightest yellow, like a new gold coin shining through the tall reeds, he left some firewood for the hermit who'd built his hut there from boughs. At a grove of pines, in spite of the fact that the evening star was already shining in the sky and our good workman was getting hungry, he paused to fill the sack of a little old woman who was trembling as she clutched her walking stick and gathered pine needles and cones from the ground. The old woman murmured, "May God bring happiness to your house!"

With still a long way to go over cleared paths that clattered like flagstones, then under high branches, then over trails of spongy moss, the bells on the mare kept tinkling in the silence and the shadows. Night was closing in when beyond a bridge made of planks that quivered over a rushing stream, but which was dry in that slow August, the village came into view amidst the groves in the valley, with the new chapel that the lord of the castle was having built for Saint Cosmas gleaming white in the shadows.

The woodcutter and his mare went into a long row of beeches, following a cart that was squeaking slowly along, all loaded down with brushwood. The stockade that once encircled the village had rotted away under the sun and rain, left in a state of abandonment during the long and bountiful years of peace as the huts rested in their orchards amidst security and plenty. Over the roofs, amply covered with thatch and secured by strips of slate, there arose the slow and aromatic smoke from the pine cones and needles that were burning abundantly in the hearths. There was the grunting of pigs in all the sties. Young girls passed along through the darkest alleys on their way to trysts, unafraid, their distaffs tucked into their waistbands. From behind the adobe walls the sleepy chorus of the whispered rosary was fading away. Every so often there was a bark from some dog on watch behind some gate or hedge. By the church the master's oven was still alight as the bounty of his bread was being baked. Next to the fountain and sheltered by the leaves of an elm was the stone bench where the elders come on Sundays to decide cases involving cattle or water rights. A pair of archers from the castle, who made their rounds in the village every night, were sleeping there, as carefree as friars, as their crossbows lay on the ground.

Moving slowly, to the measured sound of the bells, the good woodcutter and his mare reached the edge of the village, passing the tall façade of the Black Cock tavern, whose long railing, all decorated in gold, stretched out along the road. Two pilgrims with scallop shells on the coarse cloth mantels of their capes were by the door, drinking out of thick pewter tankards. Inside, a poor minstrel whose long, tangled hair fell over his ragged doublet, was plucking his three-stringed guitar and there was a mendicant friar, his rucksack on his knees, and a tinker, his brass pots and pans resting on the dark earthen floor as they rolled dice on a bench in the shadow of heavy hogsheads that all bore a white cross so that evil spirits would not sour the wine.

Our good woodcutter hurried his mare along and shortly, from a hilltop with holm oaks, he caught sight of the river in the valley below, a long, dark stream that flowed mutely under the four arches of an ancient Roman bridge that had at its center a small new chapel where a lamp flickered with a pale light in the damp mist. Farther along on the opposite bank, on the top of a long gentle slope there arose, its walls surrounded by trees, a worthy citadel, a magnificent monastery of Dominicans.

As it descended along the narrow path down the hill, the mare went tinkling along under the starry silence of the night where the way ran deep and dark between tall cliffs. And because sometimes at night a strange shepherd, his hair the color of fire and followed by a pair of tame wolves, would appear there, the good woodcutter turned his face toward the holy place where the dawn star is born and whispered the name of the angel Gabriel.

His fear now gone, he would pass through the pine grove. Only then was he treading the soil of his master's domains. Broad pastures and fields for harvesting ran down to the river that was bordered by a dark poplar grove filled with nightingales. Thereupon the castle would suddenly appear, its high walls dark and formidable. Great weathervanes in the shape of dragons and heraldic birds stood atop each tower, the bright flame of a beacon flickering on the highest.

A pavement of thick flat stones, with beech trees at the sides, led to the terrace beneath the keep where was a heavy iron-plated door at the drawbridge, always lowered in those sweet years of peace, its iron chains all rusted. To one side of the terrace there was a small shed with a roof of branches where the good white wine from the master's vineyards was sold by the bucket. The other side was gloomy, with the heavy beams of the gallows. An ancient elm shaded the stone bench where on summer afternoons the master would come to judge crimes, receive vows of homage, or lay down the tolls to be paid by merchants who would be passing through his lands with their long mule trains. No light came from the narrow slit windows of the towers. Frogs croaked in the dark waters of the moat.

Our good woodcutter passed along the long walls, where here and there a light stain could be seen, like a battle scar on a weather-beaten face, and he would pass through the high opening in a hedge that went off into the distance through the darkened fields. He went in through a narrow postern that opened in the wall in the shape of an arch and which was guarded by an enormous dog whose iron chain dragged along the paving stones.

In the area inside, within the wide walls, beyond a well with a low lip and topped by a dovecote, stood the manor house, with its simple and severe façade. The tiny lead-framed windows gave off the pale light of the long candles in the salon, alongside the ruddier light coming from the kitchens. A round turret with a balcony raised its pointed slate roof, topped by a broad weathervane in the shape of an unfurled flag. At the corners of the house, tall, thin-winged dragons turned their wide-open gullets toward the courtyard. The rainwater would pour through them into the gutters of the cistern. The lantern of a servant passing through the terrace lit up the thick row of pumpkins set out on the parapet to dry in the sun.

The good woodcutter unloaded his mare in the woodshed. Then, doffing his rabbit-fur cap, he pushed open the kitchen door that was covered with iron spikes. The fireplace, adorned with braids of onions and dried laurel branches, was so wide that on both sides of the hearth it gave shelter to long wooden benches as the bright flames from the logs burning on top of the coals illuminated the whitened walls from which hung wineskins, gleaming pots, and sacks of spices on spikes. Wearing his long leather apron and a leather cap on his close-cropped hair, the master chef was cutting meat on a huge wooden chopping block. A bare-armed servant was pouring oil from a large iron spoon over the thick chunks of meat roasting on the spits, which were longer than spears. A pair of rabbit hounds were curled up in sleep by the fire. And up against the wall, on three-legged stools, stableboys, shepherds, and ropemakers were already waiting for their supper, silent, with their caps in their hands.

A page with long, curly hair and carrying an embossed pitcher now raised the thick woolen drape in the rear that was decorated with a pair of wolf heads and that covered the broad arch of the doorway. Then the good woodcutter humbly bent his knee and caught a glimpse farther on of the manorial salon, lit up for dinner now by wax torches: the broad table was carpeted with fresh-cut herbs; the two lances that were hung over it in a cross, suspended from the ceiling by iron chains, were weighted down with thick loaves of bran; the high-backed chair at the end, crowned by a tall coat of arms, had a perch beside it upon which two falcons were dozing; there was a huge fireplace to the rear with figures in bas-relief brandishing swords. All the serfs stood up and almost immediately the fat, bald steward shuffled in on his yellow shoes of coarse cloth, bearing his clump of keys. He was the one who distributed rations to the shepherds, the ropers, the shearers, the bakers, and the other serfs on the estate who did not take their meals in the kitchens of the manor house, and very quickly the good woodcutter received in his burlap sack the bran loaf, the tankard of wine, and the slice of salted meat due on days of high court.

Once again the good woodcutter humbly and quietly pushed open the kitchen door. He passed the postern in the wall that opened onto the gardens and the bowling green. He passed along the lane of lemon trees that separated the gardens from the orchard where fountains and irrigation sluices were singing softly. He passed by the thatcher's house and the threshing floor, all bleached and freshly whitened under the light of the stars. He passed between the stables and the pages' jousting field, which went back and forth between poles that were decorated with banners all along its coarse sand track. He went out through a gate in the high fence that encircled the master's estate. Beyond it the broad meadows and pastures went down to the river where a long row of elms sheltered the castle's ropery. Another enclosure of thorny hedges encircled the bounteous rural dependencies, defended also by pitfalls for wolves, trenches with sharpened stakes, and small adobe towers with lighted lanterns.

The good woodcutter passed through the hedgerow and onto the narrow trails that led to his hut, nestled among pines and beeches on the forest's edge. It was in those groves that he worked all day. He went along that path over hills and valleys. Between the trunks of the peaceful pines the wide river flowed, brightened by the lights of the stars. The fireflies sparkled along over the tops of the thickets. The smell of honeysuckle sweetened the air.

The good woodcutter crossed a bridge of logs over a brook that was leaping over the rocks where the pages from the castle would come to fish for trout. A nightingale was singing amidst the lower branches of a poplar tree. Up ahead was an ivy-covered stone cross with a split in one arm. The good woodcutter piously removed his rabbit-skin cap. His simple heart was feeling some kind of unusual contentment that night. As he listened to the monastery bell up on the hills beyond the river tolling for Vespers, he whispered a Hail Mary with even greater devotion, certain that the Virgin was listening to him as she leaned down from Heaven, her hair adorned with all those stars that gleamed brighter than gold. In the distance now, under the pale sky, were the tops of the trees that encircled the site where his hut was hidden. His good wife, his mate, was waiting for him, spinning by the hearth. He was quickening his pace when, suddenly, out of the shadow of a weeping willow that hung over the trail, a young man with eyes that gleamed like sparks and wearing a white tunic appeared. He stood smiling before him and said: "Go joyfully into your abode, for your son will be a great saint!" And he disappeared just as suddenly. A strong smell, like that of incense mingled with cloves, spread softly through the air. The tall grasses of the meadow were fluttering and bending over as though a cape of fine silk had brushed over them.

The good woodcutter stood stock-still and motionless, all atremble in the shadows that were growing thicker and denser under the boughs of the beeches. He had trouble understanding to whom that young man with eyes brighter than altar candles had been speaking. His good companion had still not given him a son all those long years that had been so serenely spent ever since that Christmas morning when, over the snow that was gleaming in the sunshine and to the delicate song the minstrel was playing on his fiddle, he brought her, crowned with roses, to the hut he had built with his own hands with wood that those same hands had split. How could it be, then, that in their home, bereft of the merry laughter of a growing child, there would be, to their glory, a great saint? . . . His hair was standing on end as he went in under the branches, spying and listening, in hopes and in the terror of still catching some light, some sound from that strange messenger dressed in white, like the angels. The whole forest was mute and empty. Then a great fear entered his simple soul of all the invisible creatures from Heaven or from Hell rearing up in those dark places. He started to run along a narrow lane that led up to the chestnut trees that sheltered his hut. A beam of light was coming out of the door that was ajar to receive the soft coolness of the night. The watchdog who guarded it, with his spiked collar, barked happily. The good woodcutter went in, wiping away the sweat that was pouring down his face.

Sitting by the hearth on a three-legged stool, his good companion was spinning as she waited. The iron pot that hung by a chain over the fire was boiling. On a corner of the chest the glazed bowls and tin mugs were gleaming, quite clean. On the straw of the cot the coarse cotton sheet lay white and cool. Every day his mate made a great effort to keep their home neat and tidy. The woodcutter hung up his hatchet beside the chimney. Neither at supper nor as he lay next to her on the cot did he reveal to his wife his meeting with that young man with the resplendent eyes. He was fearful that she, so serious and proper, would reprimand him for his pride, why would God have sent an angel with such a miraculous message to a rude serf in a woolen wrap? It certainly had not been because of him that the young man who glowed with light had announced the sainthood of a son . . . If God had chosen them for such a blessing, it could not have been because of him, as coarse as the tree trunks in his woods, but for his good companion, so serious, so diligent in her work, pure of soul, compassionate for those poorer, always happy, and so loyal! The divine rewards were certainly for her and not for him. And as she, straight and robust, ruddy as an apple, filled the bowls with the evening meal, the woodcutter felt an opening up in his heart, like a flower that blooms again in the dew, a sweet and even deeper tenderness for the one there who for all those many years had turned their poor hut into a place where he would rather be than the rich house of the steward or the castle of his master.

ii/ It was harvest time in the vineyards of the castle's domains. Early one morning, to the song of the skylarks, as the good woodcutter was hitching his ax to his belt, ready to leave for the castle, where he would be off to split kindling wood, his helpmate, who had seated herself on the chest, her arms crossed, all serious and blushing, suddenly said, "Husband, we're going to have a child."

He stood there stock-still before her as though in the wonderment of a miracle. Then he began to babble, asking if she was sure. She was so sure that the day before, while he was working in the woods, she had gone to the monastery to receive communion so that the Holy Host would be the first food of the little child she was carrying inside her and in that way he would receive the body and blood of Jesus immediately. The good woodcutter fell mute again, as though dazzled, stroking his coarse beard. Then his good companion thought that by his silence he was grieving in his soul for that child who would come to be, like them, a serf, bound to that forest land like some oak tree, good only to serve, and when it can no longer produce it is chopped down. She remembered then that the life of service was gentle and mild on the domains of that good castellan. Old and paternal now, the good master loved his serfs and watched over them as he would the crops in his fields. So many years had passed with empty dungeons that the steward had lost the keys. Whenever the men were called to repair the roofing or clean the moats, they would come back happy and with good pay. When he would get on his mule and ride through his lands, the steward would stop to give advice to the workers and never made them remove their caps on windy days. He would keep the fees low for grinding in the master's mill or baking in his oven . . . And that fine young maiden, the heiress to those domains, where could there be found another as charitable and as kind as she? She was the one who would take her own fingers, whiter than those of our Lady, to bind up the wounds on the sheep dogs. If a windstorm carried off the thatching of a hut, she would immediately order it to be repaired. In time of severe cold she would see that old wine and sheepskins were distributed among the elderly. Since life was so easy and mild on the castle domains, they ought to be quite happy for the child that would be born to them, a contented serf in the service of those good proprietors.

"Isn't that so, husband?"

The woodcutter's face was gleaming like a piece of pure gold under a ray of sunlight.

"Blessed be God for letting me have known you, wife!"

He gave his worthy companion a strong embrace and was off to work. Smiling broadly as he went along the road leading to the castle, he was dazzled by the sky and trees. And right then and there the promise thrown out to him in the shadows of the beech trees by the young man with shining eyes was stirring up his soul. Was this then the proclaimed son who was to be a great saint? Almost frightened, he could not dare to believe in such a wonderful favor from God. A serf begetting a saint! While his master, so powerful, endowing chapels, sheltering pilgrims, who had gone off as a young man to free Jesus Christ from the evil of the Turks, had never attained the favor of a son to govern his lands, was he, a rude serf in a coarse woolen coat, a woodcutter, to be the one chosen by God to give those people the miraculous gift of a saint to protect them and to call down the friendship of the heavens? It couldn't be. Even thinking about it or hoping for it gave him the confused feeling of danger in a Pride that would offend Jesus and the other saints and thus drive off their protection for the child that was going to be born to him.

He then decided not to think any more about that promise, but when he got back to his hut at night he passed by the beeches and, to his regret, his steps slowed and he stopped to listen with his heart beating so hard that its anxious throbs were just like the ones it gives before a door closed to a treasure. The silence and the impassive darkness of the woods brought on a vague, fugitive sadness to his heart, as though a drop of cool water had dried up in his hands just as he was at his thirstiest.

As he went into the hut, however, he smiled with contentment to see his helpmate already sewing a cloth for the layette. In a corner he laid the boards he'd chosen with love along with the tools the carpenter at the castle had lent him and he began on the cradle for his son, and for both of them now everything they did or thought was completely in the service of that son who seemed so miraculous to them and so rare, like a star that suddenly bursts forth and begins to sparkle on the tip of a dry stalk. They both began to have ambitions: after rearing the child, she wanted to become the castle seamstress; he was thinking about taking the place of the chief forester, who was old and had already asked the master for retirement. When winter arrived they noticed how rude and drafty their hut was, so the good woodcutter began working on repairs every morning at first light, putting a new cover on the roof and plugging up the cracks, laying a wooden floor so that later on the child's little naked feet wouldn't feel the cold of the dark earth. Then he cleaned the yard and spread sand about, encircling it with a hedge, securing and isolating his home, which was about to enclose a treasure.

There were times when his companion would try to help him with these pious tasks, but he would not consent to it, constantly afraid that she would tire herself and thus bring harm to that precious body which, to his regret sometimes, he imagined as having been chosen by God and which he would then contemplate with awe as he would a relic in a chapel. He always gave her the largest bowl and the biggest slice of bread, because he wanted to maintain her strength and to communicate that strength to their son. He searched all through the forest for wild honey to mix with the wine, which she would drink after it was warmed at the hearth. And as the miller woman at the master's mill attended all the serf women on the castle lands at their painful hour, the poor woodcutter did all he could to serve her, bringing her sacks of pine cones, chopping her firewood, and even rolling up his woolen sleeves in an attempt to clear the water-mill. The good woman, her arms folded over her flour-covered apron, would tell him what to do. Following her instructions now, every night the good woodcutter would take a long pole and beat on the branches of the trees that gave shelter to his hut so that no owl should come to roost there, because its nighttime hooting might cause the child to be born timid and cross-eyed. His greatest care, however, was to burn some branches from a holm-oak in the hearth so that the mother's milk would be abundant and rich.

Winter arrived meanwhile, stormy and dark, and during the long sunsets as they sat on stools by the light of the hearth, those two simple serfs thought only about their child. He would count and recount in his memory all the gold pieces he'd saved over those long years and had buried under the chest, and also the others that he would still save to pay the priest-tutor who would teach his son reading and writing and Latin ... Why not? There are many sons of serfs who've sung their first mass! And as he pondered this, frightened at his incorrigible pride, he saw his son wearing a gold-encrusted miter and vestments embroidered with gold walking under a canopy along the paths of the village that were strewn with roses and anise. The mother sat silently turning her spinning wheel and could only see her little son, all chubby with his face full and smooth, pink as early morn as he lay laughing in her lap.

One night, thinking those thoughts, she fell asleep, weary and feeling lethargic from working hard all that long and warm April day. And almost immediately she saw herself sitting on the church steps in the village on a Sunday of festival, May Day: the girls were dancing about to the sound of a minstrel's fiddle; the older boys were wrestling on the grass; a serf from the castle was selling wine from a large hogshead decorated with laurel; and a knight in full armor was tethering a horse with a thick mane, so wild that no one could mount him ... And, behold, suddenly her son appears, wearing a blue doublet with a scarlet hood, like the son of a merchant, and he quickly joins the wrestling and throws the strongest boys, tames the indomitable charger, turns all the girls pale with love by simply casting his gaze on them, and then he takes the fiddle from the minstrel and starts playing so divinely that all the birds come forth out of the branches of the trees and miraculously alight on his broad shoulders. She trembled, filled with infinite pride. Then they all form a circle, raise their caps, and shout, "Look upon the one most handsome, the most skillful, and the strongest. He shall be King of the May!"

She awoke with the triumphal clamor in her ears. Her husband was whetting his ax and when, still gasping for breath, she recounted her dream; he was a long time thinking, because dreams are like tapestries, unfurled by angels, and embroidered in bright colors with the destinies yet to come.

They had both awakened that morning to a great singing of birds, so merry and so loud that it was as if all the larks and blackbirds in the forest were having a festival on the roof of their hut, while all about their bed a strange, cool smell of fresh herbs and flowers was floating. But the woodcutter's wife was unable to rise because of a weariness that was turning her paler than a linen sheet that had been laundered many times. And, amidst her moans, she begged her husband to go fetch the charitable and skillful miller woman, because her hour of glory and pain was coming. Still moaning, the good woman immediately began her prayer to Saint Margaret.

Tossing aside the ax that he carried on his leather belt, the good woodcutter ran through the fields anxiously, with little concern for the new wheat as he trampled it and leaped over the hedgerows in bloom. The miller woman was loading a full sack onto her whitened donkey. She removed the sack immediately, leaped up onto the animal, and went off at a gallop along the narrow path with the woodcutter running behind. They stopped at the door of the hut just as a pair of white doves took flight from the eaves. It was a lucky sign — and while the woodcutter went to tether the donkey in the yard, the miller woman went into the hut, first marking a cross on the ground with her foot and whispering the name of Saint Margaret. Then she came back out immediately with a broad leather strap in her hand, the one the good seamstress used to hitch up her skirts, and she shouted to the woodcutter to run to the chapel, tie the belt to the bellrope, and give it nine tolls while he recited nine Ave Marias. And there was the good woodcutter running off again holding the belt tight against his chest, like something precious. He went down by the cool of the poplars and ran along the river that was gleaming in the sunshine, where a large boat, bearing the escutcheon of an abbot and loaded down with hogsheads, was slowly making its way upstream under tow. He sped along through the marshland, where the cattle were grazing to the sound of the herders' flutes, and he hurried along the high road past the Black Cock tavern, where charcoal burners from the forest called out to him and merrily raised their tin mugs . . . he didn't hear them and continued on his way, but he had to halt suddenly because from the other end of the bridge, with the flash of arms and the gleam of bright silks, a rich cavalcade was coming along on its way to the castle. A bugle sounded, triumphant and grave, and bearded guards held their lances high. A flag unfurled its great escutcheon with bold color in the breeze. Pages covered with dust were leading pack animals burdened

down with heavy coffers painted in scarlet and gold, and a young nobleman with a black beard, up on his tall steed covered with a blue velvet
cloth, was holding a falcon on his fist and laughing with a friar who was
riding beside him on a pure-white mule. Agile greyhounds ran about
and a body of lancers followed, raising a great cloud of dust.

Bowing as he stood tight against a thorny hedge, his cap in his hand,
the good woodcutter made his humble greeting as he waited with his
heart beating anxiously. Other peasants were genuflecting next to him,
and a tall old man whispered that it was a baron from other lands who
was coming for his betrothal to the daughter of the good castellan. Then
some of the horsemen made a sudden stop. One of the pack animals,
startled, had thrown its coffers of scarlet and gold to the ground and a
steward immediately came running over, calling on all the peasants gathered there to come raise up the coffers and load the pack animal again.
And the good woodcutter went over, all upset, his eyes clouding over
with tears as he had trouble tying up the cords that secured the coffers
to the frames of the packsaddle. Three times the steward cursed him,
while his poor helpmate was suffering in return because he hadn't rung
the holy bells, which would have eased her pain!

Then the animal, loaded again, calmed down and was led away by
pages holding tight to her reins. The knights trotted along in the dust
which the sun was turning to gold. Free then, the woodcutter ran desperately to the chapel, which was being given a new coat of whitewash
by some castle serfs. With the help of the sexton, a hunchbacked old
man for whom he sometimes cut kindling wood, he tied the leather belt
to the thick bellrope and the nine holy peals soon rang happily out into
the full blue of the sky. For even greater assurance, he then lit two candles for Saint Margaret at an altar. Then, trusting in Heaven's mercy, he
went home to his hut.

As it stood there under the great trees, his eyes grew teary again as he
caught sight of the hut from the top of the hedgerow he was climbing
over. But it didn't seem as dark and humble to him now. The sun, as it
beat down on the foliage all around, had an unusual splendor. The white
cross he'd painted on the door to frighten away demons was gleaming, as
if it had been made with a bright light. An aroma sweeter than incense
was hovering over the hedges all around. The poppies in the grass were

big; the wildflowers all seemed larger, with great festive colors. Unseen springs were loudly bubbling with the fresh sound of laughter.

He was astonished by that strange beauty, never seen before on those familiar paths. And, lo, from the direction of the river, the great bells of the monastery burst forth in a festive tolling, and from the side toward the castle the chapel bell was joining in with its silver tolling into the blue. The sky was all one festive joy. And when he reached the door of his hut, the pines all around, moving their high branches, seemed to be singing.

He went in. On the cot was his helpmate, lying motionless and as white as the sheet that covered her, all tucked and smooth now. And before the flame that was fluttering in the hearth, the miller woman was huddled on a stool and holding in her lap, on a white cloth, the child . . . But the poor woodcutter, who'd been holding out his hands as if the gates of Heaven had opened before him, drew back in horror. His son was a monster!

Dark, all covered by rough, wrinkled skin, with an empty, shapeless face where the features were formed by vague, lumpy protuberances, the enormous hands clasped over his fuzzy belly, twisted legs that ended in two sharp feet, like those of a faun, all together he had the appearance of a dark root, the root of a strange tree, still dark from the dark earth out of which it had been torn. And not a cry. It had the rudiments of a vegetable thing!

Two slow and bitter tears rolled down over the good woodcutter's beard. He took a step over to the edge of the cot. Across the deathlike white face of his companion tears were also running in the bitterness of a dream undone.

Since that deformed creature was certainly going to die, his father himself, terrified and weeping, baptized him and gave him the name of Christopher.

For three days and three nights Christopher neither suckled nor cried, motionless in the cradle over which the woodcutter and his mate kept constant watch with stubborn hope as they sensed the heat of strong blood under that hard, wrinkled skin. One evening when both had dozed off from fatigue, they suddenly heard an odd sound rise up out of the sheets in the cradle that was now rocking, something like the slow bleating of a robust lamb. Christopher was opening his eyes, and they finally got a look at them, of a pale blue, like the flower of a periwinkle. The mother, radiant, clutched him to her breasts, which the abundance of milk had been suffocating, and with only a few long and deep sucks, Christopher emptied one of them.

From that moment on he began an intense and rapid existence. When he slept his breathing was stronger than the wind in the trees. When he awoke his cries shook the hut, and his ceaseless and voracious hunger dried up his mother's milk. He would then suck large chunks of wild honey strained through a cloth and would lie nibbling on the finger his father would place between his gums, as hard as stone, to calm him down.

In the meantime, that monstrosity with the look of a thick, dark root began to take on the shape of a coarse but human body. His skin, having lost its dark roughness, was smooth and red, like the skin of an apple. His head emerged from between his shoulders as though it had made the decision to begin life, and his legs, straight now and with two great flat feet, were so strong that when he moved them he came close to up-setting the cradle.

It was not very long before he was too big for the cradle, which fright-ened his mother. It was during the heat of the month of May, so the good woodcutter took some dry moss, covered it with a cloth, and made a bed in the garden, where they could lay him down under a flowering mimosa tree. But Christopher would roll off the mattress seeking the warm, soft ground, where he would lie and stretch out in delight, as though in his preferred element, giving a soft, mute smile that was already showing the glimmer of a tooth. At that moment a flight of butterflies with prodigious colors, the like of which the woodcutter had never seen, flew over the vegetable patch. A rosebush that had withered a year ago, showing only a dry stalk, burst forth with large roses that perfumed all the air around them. The blackbirds that gathered there with their incessant festive noise would fall silent when the baby slept, clenching his great fists. The mimosa and all the other trees began to spread their branches out like sheltering canopies over the spot where the mattress was laid. And one day as his mother began to open the door to the yard she was startled by the sight of a large deer on the other side of the hedge, his tall antlers in the foliage, gazing down on Christopher with the gravity of a grandfather.

He was so heavy by then that the good woman would double over, barely able to carry him from the door to his cradle, and yet he was only six months old. The miller woman, who would stop by with her beast loaded down with sacks to have a look at him, was surprised at his ruddy color, his strength, his perfectly formed limbs, and by that calm way he would stay all through a long summer day, his bluish eyes lifeless and bereft of gleam and fastened on a single stone or a single branch. And in that transformation she saw a miracle by Saint Anne.

Long before Christmas Christopher began to walk. He was soon running about the yard and was almost as tall as the hedge. And when he had to grab hold of a branch to steady himself, it would crack, just as it would beneath the force of a strong man. His father was living in enchantment and fascination at that magnificent strength, and his greatest pleasure was to see the child lift a heavy iron pot or go over to the fireplace carrying two big pieces of firewood. He had no doubts but that his son would be the strongest man on all the castle lands, and he was already imagining him as a soldier in thick armor commanding the regiments of the castle. In the mother's heart there was a kind of mute, vague sadness over that miraculous growth in strength and figure. She could no longer carry him in her arms. Christopher was only a year old and he was no longer her little boy, her tiny child. The tender cares of her motherhood were no longer of any use to him. She no longer had to watch over his steps or put food into his mouth. Enormous, as strong as she, Christopher, when he was hungry, could lift the lid off a pot or split the toughest loaves of bread in half. The woodcutter would mark a white line on the wall at Christmastime to show his son's height, and the marks kept getting higher and higher, almost to the level of the shelf for dishes. At the age of two his little head, covered with a thick golden fleece, already reached up to the woodcutter's waist. The little linen skirts she had sewn for him with so much love were lying useless at the bottom of the chest, without his ever having been small enough to appear in them on Sundays, holding her hand in front of the village church. And when she saw him, still as mute and innocent as a nursing child, but now so large that he almost filled the doorway of the hut where it was his habit to spend hours standing monotonously gazing at the sky and the sunshine, his poor disconsolate mother would feel a tear wetting her cheek.

What consoled her was the sense that he was so gentle and mild. If she became frightened and would take away the woodcutter's ax, which he liked to raise, and pull him away from the fire, which was a constant attraction for him, he didn't show the least resistance or annoyance. A bale of woolen cloth could not be more inert. He would spend long hours just where he sat, or in the shade of the cherry tree in the yard. He took delight in watching his mother spin, completely taken with the turning and the squeaking of the spindle. And he would give her hand a mute, quiet touch as though asking for it never to stop. Then she would hug him to her breast and whisper despairingly.

"Why aren't you smaller?"

And yet, already almost four years old, he still hadn't spoken. The only sound that came out, hollow and thick, from between his lips that were the color of dawn, was a Hunh! If he was thirsty he would point with a big finger and snort Hunh! If he wanted to go out he would point to the door and grunt, with empty eyes, at his mother, Hunh! Hunh! The poor woman had already lost her sweet hope of ever hearing him say Mother or Father. She had no doubts now that she had conceived a mute, an imbecile, and in her sorrow — and with a remnant of pride — she would not permit Christopher to go beyond the hedge around the yard, or go down to the roadway, afraid that workers in the forest or the neighbor women in the village would come across him and discover his monstrosity and be sorry for the sadness in that home.

What frightened her more than anything else, though, was the thought of Christopher's insensibility to pain as something diabolical. A wasp would sting him on the face and he wouldn't cry nor would his skin swell up. Whether on a cool bed of moss or on a thorny bramble, he would sit down indifferently. And one day he stuck his hand in some boiling water and withdrew it calmly, as though it were made of stone.

"Alas, my husband," the poor mother would mutter, "What kind of a miracle is this one that we've been given?"

Her husband would sigh mournfully. All that joy of his over that early robust figure of their son, so promising, had become a constant grief over his deformity, for Christopher couldn't speak. He had the simplicity of a small animal as he lay in the cradle, but he already came up to his father's shoulder and was just as strong as he, with large muscles and formidable hands that would brandish an ax in the air as though it were a small stick of elm wood. The woodcutter no longer mentioned his son to the other serfs of the castle, charcoal burners, sawmen, comrades in the forest. If only Christopher could at least talk, with that stature of his he would have had the semblance of a man . . . He could have gone with him to his work, wouldn't have shown his age, but would have appeared to be a strong young comrade who shared his home. But the way he was, huge, with a wide face and the shoulders of an athlete, he spent hours scratching on the ground like a small child, crawling about as he observed the scurrying ants or sitting quietly in a corner sucking a finger.

In the village already among the serfs of the castle, word was going about that the woodcutter's son was a monster. It most certainly must have been some sorcerer, an enemy of his, who had cast such a fearsome fate upon him. And some, the bolder ones, would come nosing around and spying on Christopher's hut in order to get a look at the bewitched boy. One afternoon the poor mother heard coarse laughter coming from nearby the garden hedge and she guessed that curiosity seekers had come to mock the sorrow of her home. Now, she always kept the door to her hut closed. Before, she had kept it so chaste and clean and had allowed in the gaze of anyone along with the sun's rays. When some woman friend from the village or some servant girl from the castle would call her from outside, before opening the gate she would push her poor monster off into the shadows of the trees, and he would go over there, dragging his feet and drooling out of the corner of his mouth. She would have liked to have walled in all of their dwelling with a high board fence to cut it off from all the world about. And at the same time it pained her to have to confine poor Christopher to those few square feet of hut and garden, keeping him hidden like some cursed offspring of whom she was ashamed. Her whole simple, upright soul was drowning in sadness and gloom. And she no longer had any doubts but that her son's monstrosity was the punishment the Virgin Mary had given her for her motherly pride, so certain had she been that her Christopher would be divinely beautiful, just like the Christ Child that Saint Joseph was holding in his arms, and it had scandalized the Virgin deep in the heart of Heaven. And quite justly so! How could the fruit of a servile womb be equal in beauty to the fruit of a divine one?

One afternoon as she was having such thoughts and twirling her spindle, she heard a sound in the yard, something like stones crashing through the foliage of the cherry tree. Worried, she unbolted the door and caught sight of three pages from the castle behind the hedge, merry and cruel, making fun of her son and throwing stones and dry clods at him as they would at an animal in its lair. And Christopher, stronger than the pages but not understanding, was just sitting there, motionless, in the center of the yard on the paving stones as he held his hand over his face. She snatched him desperately inside and slammed the door as the pages, offended by the serf woman's boldness, pelted the walls of the hut with stones. From that day on the poor mother began to waste away. It was a dull sadness, a sorrow over everything, which would leave her not moving through long afternoons, her distaff forgotten in her waistband and her spindle fallen to the floor. She was drowsy and lost in a endless, nameless melancholy. All manner of work had become a heavy burden for her, like something useless. It had become an almost impossible chore for her to dress Christopher, who still had not learned how to put on his jerkin, and who would very nearly cause his poor mother to blush, with his naked body that was as large as hers, and which to her eyes had the look of a naked stranger, some man that had invaded her home. At night, pale and silent, she would push her bowl of soup away and Christopher would then devour it in silence. And she had no wish for her concerned husband to summon the castle physician. What for? "My sickness," she would mutter, "is just going to grow and grow . . ." Evenings in the hut were as gloomy as those in hospital. So weak that she was unable to get out of bed, she would contemplate her husband sitting beside her with a long, nostalgic gaze, the tearful gaze of someone about to go away. As he held her hands he kept insisting that she try one of the remedies the miller woman had advised for the wasting of her body, and just to keep him happy she consented to let him tie a sack with a frog in it around her neck and to drink a broth made of daisies picked during a full moon. But there was no pain, no agony as her poor body just seemed to be disappearing, so thin and transparent that she could see the red glow of the hearth fire through the palm of her hand.

From the time when she first fell ill, Christopher had not left her bedside, anxious for his mother and stupefied as if from his effort to understand why she was lying there with sleepy eyes while the sun enwrapped the hut and even the trees had awakened. At times he would touch her arms, her shoulder, and come out with a sad little moan. She would whisper with all the spirit she could muster, "My poor boy! My poor boy!" But then she would turn her head away with bitterness as she saw him go off, with the slow, awkward steps of a trained bear, to pick up the heavy jug of water with one hand and empty it in one swallow.

It was the end of autumn by then. The woodcutter had come home and was shaking out his heavy jacket, wet with the dampness of the forest. From time to time a strong wind would moan in the pine groves. The lamp had been burning all night long. On a pallet beside the hearth, Christopher was sleeping under some goatskins, a huge shape in the shadows, and breathing as heavy as a bellows in a forge. With her husband sitting beside her on a stool, the poor woman, numb with fatigue and insufficient sleep, lay awake thinking about the sadness and lack of care from which that poor hut, where she'd made such a delightful nest, was suffering! Who was going to prepare her husband's soup? Who was going to take care of that poor monster who didn't even know how to button his jacket? A great sob shook her thin breast and the woodcutter, waking up, confused, adjusted the blanket on the cot and went to stir the coals in the fireplace.

One night, when there was a great silence among the trees and in the air because snow was falling, she felt a great cold pass over her face, and from the faintness that was taking hold of her she reached out her hand and felt she was about to say goodbye forever to her man. And her slow, empty eyes then met those of her Christopher, who had risen, wrapped in a goatskin, and who was standing by the cot, alert and, as though waiting, frightened. She moved her lips to ask him to go back to bed, to keep warm, but all she could get out was a sigh, in the midst of a faint … And it seemed to her that before her very eyes her son was starting to grow, visibly, his red hair touching the ceiling of the hut already as the roof opened up and Christopher kept on growing through the hole, up to the sky, taller than the pine trees, his face lost now amidst the snow-flakes, and so ugly and monstrous that the stars were fleeing across the sky, their souls all affrighted. She gave a cry. The poor woodcutter woke up immediately and fell across her, trembling. His helpmate appeared asleep. Then Christopher came slowly over to the cot and as he laid his hands softly on her sweat-dampened hair, he shouted,

"Oh! Mama, Mama, don't you go to sleep!"

Christopher had spoken! Her son had talked! A blush of infinite contentment came over her weather-beaten face as it remained motion-less, but smiling, and the good old woman departed this earth for the beyond …

iv/ The tree in the yard was full of cherries. The woodcutter was working in the forest once more, starting with the first song of the lark, and the widow of a charcoal burner from the woods came every day to take care of the hut and look after Christopher. She was a scrawny, somber old woman, who would emerge from the pine grove leaning on a staff and accompanied by a black cat. During the first days, hunched over the fire or weaving by the door, she would keep casting her beady little eyes from under thick, bushy brows nervously on Christopher's huge arms and legs. That misshapen creature, whom his father would simply call "the boy," and whom she was there to take care of, filled her with fright as he would lift the huge jug filled with water to his mouth or as he stood filling the doorway to the garden and sucking his fingers as he stared at the sun. In spite of the woodcutter's assurance that he was quite gentle, only simple-minded, she was afraid of that mute gentleness, just as she would have been of a dark, silent lair from which a wild beast was about to emerge. But when she watched him all day long resting quietly under the cherry tree, smiling at the ants climbing up his now-hairy legs or sitting cross-legged in the yard sucking on a finger and pondering as he stared at the wheel she was turning, the old woman recognized his simplicity and began to look upon him as some domestic animal, a fat pig or donkey, that belonged to the place. In order not to feel those dull, bluish eyes resting on her, to see that huge body cluttering up the hut blocking the light, she would push him out into the yard and there, when the bells struck noon, she would bring him his soup and ration of pone in a large bowl, which she would set down on the ground. And Christopher would spend his days there sitting, pushing the earth about with his slow, vague fingers, listening to the rustle of the leaves, or moving with slow steps over to the hedge and extending his wondering dull gaze out over the fields to the distant groves, with the slow quiet of a well-fed ox. The sawyer woman in the meantime would sweep the floor, scour the utensils in the cupboard with sand, beat the mattress from the cot, or would sit by the door and spin until, at the Angelus, the bells on the white mare that the good woodcutter was leading by the bridle could be heard coming up the path.

Then the old woman would shake hands at the door and tell how Christopher had been so quiet and good, playing in the yard or listening to the stories she knew about fairies and Moors. The woodcutter would stroke his beard in contentment and Christopher, by the hearth where the wood was piled up, would smile in wonderment, shaking his earth-covered hands.

When cold weather arrived, the sawyer woman, working inside the hut, would sometimes moan and rub her knees. Christopher would gaze at her with compassion in his eyes. One day, when she was limping and moaning even louder as she went out to the spring, Christopher timidly put his hand on the rim of the thick earthen jug and whispered, all ablush, "I'll go." Startled, she released it and stood by the door watching Christopher disappear among the elms and come back up the path in the cold rain, carrying the jug in his extended arm, for which it weighed less than a small pitcher. He was smiling broadly with great contentment. The old woman dried his wet hair and, for the first time since she'd been taking care of him, she treated Christopher like a human being. She spoke about the aches in her poor bones, of her husband, who had left her in her old age without bread, and about Death, who was drawing closer with his great scythe. But the face that Christopher would lift up to her as he squatted by the fireplace went back to that immobility, without soul or warmth, of a face made of stone. And it was to her old cat, whom she'd taken onto her lap, and not to Christopher that the sawyer woman went on silently about the complaints of her old age. On that afternoon, however, Christopher swept the hut with the broom that the limping and groaning old woman put in his hands.

And from then on, little by little, he began doing all the household chores. All through the long winter the sawyer woman no longer moved from her corner by the fireplace, but stayed spinning at her wheel with the cat curled up by her feet. Christopher would go fill the pitcher at the spring, light the fire in the hearth, scrub the pot, clean the cutlery in the cupboard, beat the mattresses from the cots, and on Saturdays even wash the clothes in a tub of hot water and ashes. And to all these services he gave a thorough application and a deep interest. His huge body was becoming more agile, quicker all over. Now from the thick lips that once had only opened in a witless and dead smile, living murmurs came, "That's good! That came out good . . . Christopher cleaned it!"

At supper that night as he slowly crumbled his cornbread into his soup, the woodcutter studied his Christopher with amazement as he now seemed different to him, more alert and alive, aware that his father cut trees in the forest, that the white mare and the land and the live-stock that grazed there belonged to a master, and that on Sundays you rested and visited God in his house as the bells sang out into the air. But what most fascinated the good woodcutter was Christopher's new care in serving him, a desire that had suddenly been born in his heart without anyone's planting it there. As soon as he heard him coming up through the fields he would go, with his slow, rocking gait, and take the reins of the mare, then lead her to the corral, where the straw had been cut and the trough was full of water. In the hut, down on his knees, he would loosen the laces of the heavy leather boats that were covered with mud and he would spread out the dirty old woolen coat, all wet with the dampness of the forest, before the fireplace. The good woodcutter would whisper, with the radiance of the luckiest person in the world, "It was God sent you, my son!" and in the eyes with which Christopher was smiling at him, he could catch, in spite of its being crude and simple, a light, an unusual glow. His innocent boy was thinking now, under-standing now. Still pale and hesitant, but certain and completely visible, a small soul was budding in that huge body, like a small light in a great tower.

After dinner, taking advantage of the oil left in the lamp, the wood-cutter now had the wonderful contentment of chatting with his son as he had done before with his good helpmate, talking about his hard day in the woods, the tree he'd cut down, the timber provided the monastery, and the complaints of the sawyers about his honor, the steward. The poor home had lost the cold silence that up till then had caused him to swallow his soup in sadness, to lie down on his widowed cot with such melancholy that even the swaying branches of the cork trees sounded to him like human moans. Now he had a companion and he could start growing old in happiness.

Then he took pride in his son and wanted those in the village to know him. Christopher was still growing, and already before he was ten he had both the body of a large man and great strength, even though there was still no fuzz on his smooth and beardless face, but he had the innocence of a child even if it was one as tall as the hedge was high. Red curly hair covered his small head like a tight woolen cap, down to the back of his neck and over his thick brows. The muscles on his face jutted out, firm and wide, like those of a bull. His wide mouth kept on getting wider with a smile of innocence and surprise for everything. And his little eyes, as tiny as blue beads, spread a sweetness out over everything with a slow, compassionate caress. His broad limbs all moved with a timid slowness, even when going down to the spring or passing along the garden hedge. He was accustomed to carrying a stick on which he would rest his huge hands when he stood still, and he would lay his heavy chin, marked with a deep dimple, on them. The tailor for the castle pages cut a pilgrim's cloak from a piece of blue camlet that his father had kept in the chest for a long time, and also a doublet, straight as a sack, which was tied at the waist with a leather cord and fell down in folds over scarlet boots that were sewn with a relief of yellow cordovan. Clothed and clean like that, like the son of a merchant, every Sunday his father, smiling with pride, would take him down along the pathways to mass in the village.

Christopher would enter the old church, whose austere walls were like those of a citadel, with perplexity and a vague fear. He knew that the tall stone house there, with glittering lights, was that of our Lord God, who had one just like it in every village where, on the quiet, silent days when no work was done, the people, dressed in fresh clothes, would come to visit and praise him. And ever since that Sunday in May when he came down from the hut, through green fields and between hedges of woodbine to hear his first mass, that house of our Lord God had held for him in his simple soul the terror of a place that was very rich, very sad, and full of mystery. The great cold shadow that fell from the dark arches and the way the images, pale and emaciated, on the altars seemed to be suffering; the naked lad with his twisted body, tied to a tree and run through with arrows; the queen so sad under her golden crown, in her satin cloak, her heart run through by seven swords; the monk who gleamed like silver showing the wounds in his open hands. In candela-bras wrought in gold the flames of sadness were burning. Clothes of velvet, silk, with the glint of embroidery were covering recesses from where something like the murmur of a moan would emerge sometimes. The people would all lower their faces to the stone floor, full of sad thoughts. And a strip of light from a crack in the wall lighting up the greatest sadness of all, the Man, fastened to a cross with nails and with fresh blood on his knees, his chest, and his feet as he lifted up his tormented face to Heaven and seemed to be crying out in his abandonment. This, then, is what the house of the Lord was like, full of golden objects, flowing blood, magnificent velvets, sadness, and silence!

Meanwhile, before the main altar a completely bald old man in a resplendent cape was reaching out his arms, kissing the embroidered altar cloth, turning the pages of a large book, holding up a wafer made from very white flour, and drinking from a cup embedded with glittering jewels. Facing him alongside his father was Christopher, kneeling on the stone floor like his father, drawing a cross on his forehead, pounding his chest with his hard fist. But he was left feeling alien to the adoration that was unfolding before him, like the dark stone pillar against which he was leaning, weary from that melancholy of the house of God. His eyes then became absorbed by the large white dove that stood motionless with its wings spread above the tabernacle and which every Sunday attracted him most, always there, faithful, patient, with neither of its legs trembling. She alone was sweet, happy, and natural like other doves, adorable and pleasant to see, with her beak, pink legs, and neither blood nor gold on her dove's body. She alone didn't frighten or dazzle him, and Christopher couldn't understand why she stayed there in those cold shadows and amid those granite stones next to agonies and pains; why didn't she fly off and go cooing with the others in the chestnut trees in the churchyard? His wandering thoughts then turned to the meadows through which he'd passed as he came down from the hut to the green coolness of the poplars and into the sun that warmed the lizards sleeping on the white stones. He most certainly would have liked to have stayed there in the fields by the riverbank all that long Sunday, feeling the cool grass between his knees, running his hands over the freshness of the lower branches. But on Sundays you had to visit and praise our Lord God. Only in that way, as his father maintained, would he go up to Heaven later. He would surely go up to Heaven one day. But an uneasiness passed through his soul because Heaven, like the church, he imagined to be dark and gloomy, with gold figures, great silken cloths, men covered with blood, queens with their poor hearts run through by swords. A place high up, very rich and very sad. How much better was the garden where he lived, with the cherry tree, the hedge of woodbine, and parsley beside the vintage tub! A murmur passed among the stone pillars; all the faces became smiling, brighter. The steward was coming down from his seat: the Mass had ended. And contentment filled Christopher's heart as he saw the chestnut trees in front of the church once more.

Then, little by little, the forests and the fields became more familiar to him. He would now run his thick hand over the softness of the mosses. He would climb up the trunks of trees to peek inside the thickness of their foliage. He would lie down in the tall grass and roll his curly hair through the whiteness of the daisies. And at the same time he was discovering in all this Nature a multiple, broad, active, and miraculous life. The earth he would crumble in his thick fingers was soft from the worms that inhabited it. Every blade of grass sheltered a colony of insects, more numerous than the people in the village on Sundays under the chestnut trees by the church. Every leaf covered a wing. In the underbrush long, hairy backs would rub against his slow legs. Shiny little eyes peeked out from the blackness of their burrows; the crack of the bushes announced the passage of wild things. A confused, obscure love for all those creatures was growing in his simple heart. He would spend enchanted hours lying in the grass on the bank of a clear pool admiring the long-legged insects that skated across the smooth water. With his hands, smiling, he would summon all the deer that would suddenly appear on the edge of clearings, displaying their majestic and solemn faces among the trunks of the chestnut trees. And he would pause on trails that were green with dampness and moss to stroke the backs of toads.

In that way the forest was becoming familiar and intimate for Christopher, and he would spend days in its deepest nooks, buried in the greenery, leaning against a rock, or lying prone above a pool of water, not moving, vegetating in the infinite sweetness of feeling his long hair entangled in the leaves, his shoulders warmed by the same sun that was beating down on the stones. Frogs leaped across his feet as they would over half-buried tree trunks in the damp grass. Only hunger made him return to the hut. It was difficult for him to pick up his feet, as though he had already taken root. He smelled of earth and dampness all over his body, and in the evening shadows it was as if he were a log breaking away from other logs. He'd grown so prodigiously that he had to stoop to go through the door of the hut. As no stool supported his weight now, he would sit on the floor by the hearth at the feet of his father, who was all taken with awe and amazement at that strength there.

When the good woodcutter left for the woods he no longer told him, "Christopher, don't leave the yard because something bad might happen to you." And then gradually he began to explore farther, marveling at the meadows, the riverbanks, and the dense groves upon which he had so often extended his wondering vague gaze. Slow and uncertain, like a straying sheep, he went down along the open pathways that were bordered by hedges, stopping with every other step to stare in amazement at the fields of tall wheat, the broad meadows, sleek and pleasant to the eye, like green velvet all alive with daisies, poppies, and crowfoot. Cutting through the poplar he would go to admire for long, mute hours the flow and gleam of the great river, or he would go in under the pine trees where, vague and thoughtful, he would forget himself until dusk and love the coolness, the silence, breathing in with amazement the aroma of the pine pitch. Then he would slowly return to the hut, his arms hanging loosely down, his face to the breeze, smiling and content.

At night he would dream of the soft branches that caressed his face, the clear, cool water that flowed away singing between his naked feet buried in the sand. And when morning came, throwing the wooden bolt to the hut, he would go down to the fields. All through his heart there coursed something like a wish to embrace in one intimate hug all the land that he saw, from the wildflowers along the paths to the vast forest that, magnificent and somber, covered the hillsides. But there was a kind of timidity in him, a bashfulness that held him back from even touching the mulberries.

v The pages, who would come to the fountain to jolly with the girls, spoke about him in the evenings when they would all gather at the castle, and the castellan expressed a desire to see him. One morning, therefore, followed by his father, who had dressed him up in his best clothes, he went up the hill on the way to the drawbridge. Two halberdiers in leather kilts stood guard at the gate and the mastiffs in the courtyard pulled furiously on the chains restraining them, lifting up their forelegs and barking at the giant as he passed. The castle façade rose up majestically with its tall arched portal over some marble steps. There were two towers with peaked roofs at the corners, covered with overlapping tiles. Every window held a yellow flowerpot with a carnation plant.

A page led Christopher up the tall stairway and, after raising up a tapestry, left him in a room with an arched ceiling where a large log was burning in a tall hearth and where the tips of lances propped up against the cold bare wall were gleaming. A pale greyhound entered, leaping and running about, followed by the castellan and a lady, and after them some pages and a priest with a breviary in his hand. The Master's lean body was covered by a velvet tunic fringed in fur that fell down over his pointed shoes, also fur-trimmed. His red beard, stiff and pointed, stood out over a nose that was like a vulture's beak. As his curly hair fell back from under his velvet cap, it looked like a shaggy pomegranate tree. The lady's tall headdress almost touched the top of the doorway as her dark gown dragged along the flagstones, and her lowered eyes seemed to be contemplating her fallen crossed hands, paler than wax, from which a rosary hung. There was a jester alongside them, a humpbacked dwarf who held his hand on the ungainly hilt of a wooden sword with burlesque pride.

Christopher's father dropped to his knees and, as Christopher remained standing with his cap tucked under his arm, his father pulled on his coattail for him to kneel, too. Over them the Master, tugging at his thick beard, the lady, with a timid smile, and the chaplain, with his hands crossed over his belly, were contemplating Christopher's huge limbs. At a command from the Master he stood up and took a step. The Master felt his muscles, even tugged his crisp curly hair. Then, at another command, three men brought in a huge, rusty iron sword that looked like the mace of Hercules. With an easy movement Christopher brandished it in the air. Then the jester pulled out his wooden sword and advanced on Christopher with the gestures of a duelist. The bells on his bonnet jingled, his hump twisted grotesquely, and with a thin little voice he shouted, "En garde! God's will be done!" Thereupon Christopher lowered his iron sword as his mouth opened up to reveal a great cave out of which came an enormous, thundering, resonant laugh that rattled the glass panes in their lead frames. The lady put her pale hands to her ears, the pages in the rear muffled their laughter, and with a wave of his hairy hand the Master ordered them to take Christopher down to the kitchens.

Below, in the kitchens, great chunks of meat on spits were roasting over a huge fire that was crackling in the tall fireplace, while in pots that hung from iron chains the boiling water was making the lids rattle. The cooks were rolling dough with the whitened rolling pins. A jet of water was singing in the stone basin and two aged chambermaids were sitting on their stools spinning by the window where the basil grew. A servant brought in a huge glazed bowl in which a large wooden spoon had been plunged into a thickness of vegetables and slices of meat. Christopher devoured it with his head down, but then from the dark entry way that led below came the sounds of grunts from men making an effort to carry a rather heavy load, so Christopher put down the spoon, and after wiping his mouth with the back of his hand he disappeared down through the dark archway. He returned a moment later carrying on his back a broad hogshead reinforced with iron hoops. Behind him came two men still wiping away their sweat and all bent over. To repay Christopher, the cook offered him a tureen filled with wine, which he drank slowly, holding it with both hands and with his eyes closed.

Then, picking up his fur cap, he left. The chambermaids ran to the windows to have a look at him; from up on the battlements the men at arms leaned over. And he walked along, confused, slowly scratching his head.

Meanwhile, winter was coming on, and the roadways were turning white with snow as birds were falling down dead from the naked branches of the trees. One afternoon Christopher's father returned home from the forest looking pale, and he sat down in the doorway to watch the setting sun at the end of the valley. Christopher was sitting in front of him and clumsily putting a blade onto the handle of a scythe. When the sun had disappeared he heard a moan behind him and he turned to see his father with his head against the side of the house and his hand over his heart. All that night Christopher's wails thundered up and down through the village. His father's corpse was laid out on the ground under a sheet, and in the doorway that he filled with his vast hulk, Christopher was sobbing with great shrieks.

For two days and two nights Christopher lay by the door with his face against the ground. At times he would shake all over with sobbing, and then his huge shape would become as motionless as the great logs lying all around, felled and rigid. Winter and hunger had brought wandering famished people along the roads who attacked huts. One band sneaked up one of those nights, coming in through an open window and stealing everything inside, clothes, tools, the grain in the chest, and even the bedding on the cot, while Christopher lay prostrate and snoring slowly, with the sound of a gushing river in the darkness.

That morning, when he saw the empty hut, Christopher chopped down a young poplar, cleaned off all the branches, and leaning on the long trunk, went off up into the hills and disappeared.

vi/

For a year he lived up in the mountains, and gradually, in that solitude far away from all human life, he came close to losing his humanity and was like a chunk of the mountain that was all around him. As he would sit motionless for days, his thick, rough limbs appeared indistinguishable from the rocks, and the same gale winds that rustled the branches of the trees disheveled his hair. When he raised his voice, it mingled with the roar of the torrents. Wild creatures were not afraid of him. Birds would roost on his arms the same as they would on the branches of trees. The mountain was secluded. A hermit had lived there once, but his penance had laid him low. An angel came down to fetch him up, and the hut he'd lived in fell apart, board by board, under the winter rains. For a whole year no human gaze had fallen on Christopher, nor had any human voice brought joy to his heart.

He had almost forgotten humankind, and all that remained in his simple spirit, quite confused, was a memory of families, homes, and children laughing behind hedges. He would spend his days without making any movement, only looking about him. Sometimes he would move an arm with the slow motion of a branch shaken by the breeze. When thunder would roll, he would lift his face to the sky for an instant but then fall back into his immobility.

One day, however, he heard the tinkle of bells and the sound of voices, and from behind some boulders came a string of loaded mules that some armed men were leading. As night was falling, the men halted in a clearing, and a short time later there was a bright fire burning, mats were laid on the ground, and the men were sitting in a circle and passing a tankard of wine from hand to hand. Christopher spent the whole night spying on them from the woods, and he became infinitely curious, with an urge to listen to their talk from close by, drink out of their tankard, and warm himself by their bright fire. If they wished, he could lead one of the pack mules. A strange, odd impulse came over him, making him admire those men, and all night long he kept watch so that wild beasts would not attack their camp.

32

In the morning they rolled up their mats and the long mule train went on down the slope. The tinkling bells were lost in the defiles. Then a strange cold, a cold that he didn't understand, which wasn't coming from the wind or the snow, chilled Christopher right through his heart. And through his simplicity he sensed that he wouldn't feel so cold if he could hear human voices again or the footsteps of loaded pack animals, or the crackle of a campfire lit by human hands.

Then he began to explore the mountain, all the ravines, gulleys, valleys, woods, and crags that he knew. And the feeling of coldness began biting into him more and more, so much so that he felt completely exhausted. He held his head in his hands and great tears rolled down his cheeks. Afternoon was on its way out and night was coming on, all full of stars, and Christopher, motionless, could sense through his tears that things that had disappeared were rising up like visions: a old woman loaded down with firewood and bending over under her burden, children unable to cross a river, a team of oxen that couldn't pull a cart loaded with stones. And a strong urge came over him to work, to carry the old woman's load, to help the team of oxen. He picked up his staff and began to descend the mountain.

vii /

One afternoon the women at the spring saw something that looked like a tower approaching. The younger ones fled in fright, but others, older, raised up their hands and said, "It's Christopher! It's Christopher!"

His vast body had grown even larger and his red mat of hair was higher than the tallest trees. Slow in his movements, each one of his steps seemed to have trouble detaching itself from the ground. He smelled of sod and of trees, and a red beard, with a kind of singed curly hair, covered his face, while his blue eyes still held a look of perpetual wonderment, like those of a child.

When he reached the spring he lowered his head, drank slowly, then, wiping his lips, he looked at the women with a pleasant smile and they, their fear gone now, recognized the son of the woodcutter as they gathered around him, their tall hats touching his knee, and raised their astonished eyes up to the heights of his face.

His obtuse mind didn't recognize any of them but he kept on smiling. Through the dense shadows of his spirit certain memories must have slowly risen up, however, of the times when he was still young and a serf of the village, and his huge arms moved slowly, as if seeking new bundles to pick up or weaknesses to assist. Almost immediately upon seeing an old woman passing by, bent down under a bundle of firewood, Christopher took it from her and placed it under his arms as though it were one simple log. Then, as a passing cart was so loaded down with stones that the oxen could not pull it, he unhitched the animals and picked up the shaft. Next, after spotting the miller prodding his old donkey loaded with sacks of flour, he took his five enormous fingers and lifted the sacks off the animal. After that he lifted up to his shoulders a crippled old man who could barely drag himself along. And just like that, the bundle of firewood under his arms, the old man hanging about his neck, the sacks of flour hanging from his hand, the cart with the heavy stones pulled by his other arm, he began walking toward the village, followed by the women with others waving at him from doors along the way and shouting, "It's Christopher! It's Christopher!"

Free of his burdens, he went to sit down by the stone cross in front of the church, where his head reached up to the chest of the crucified Jesus and seemed to be resting on him. In the meantime people, the whole village, came running up to have a look at Christopher. Men came out of the tavern wiping their lips, women kept on sewing as they came, while others still carried greens for the soup in their hands. The children, frightened at first, then saw that he was holding out his hand to them with a pleasant smile so they leapt up onto it and sat there laughing and waving their caps as though up on a balcony. The land warden finally came over and stood before Christopher, rolling his wide eyes, scratching his chin, and speaking softly to the halberdier who followed him, mistrustful no doubt of those strong muscles capable of demolishing the village, stealing everything, and vanquishing the halberdiers.

None of his fetters was surely strong enough to manacle those enormous wrists on which the children were climbing just as they would on the thick branches of an elm tree. So he moved off with dignity, still stroking his pointed beard. Then a pair of mules brayed down the road and two brother guardians from the monastery appeared, who, having no doubt heard about him, had turned off the road to have a look at the huge giant. The women all curtseyed and the men, their caps in their hands, lowered their eyes. Then the older brother prodded his mule with his heel until he brought it closer to Christopher in order to test his suspicion that Satan might be present in such a huge body, and he made the sign of the cross and whispered the name of Jesus three times. Christopher then made the sign of the cross on his forehead. The guardian then began to walk around him calmly, then spoke in a low voice to his companion who was giving a reverent smile of approval. Finally the guardian shouted out, "Christopher, if you would like to earn your bread, come to the door of the monastery tomorrow morning at matins."

The two friars prodded their mules and were off. People gradually returned to their homes from which smoke was now rising from the lighted hearths. One by one, the stars began to shine. And Christopher, all alone and weary, lay down beside the stone cross, where the sexton had come to light the lamp.

Lying on his back Christopher gazed at the stars. They were the same ones he'd contemplated so many times in the mountains, but they seemed brighter, closer, and to be giving off a warmth like the lamps that lit a human dwelling. And in the end he imagined himself emerging from those cottages lit up all around and sending their smoke up into the sky with a warmth that penetrated him right into his heart. He fell asleep with a smile on his face.

Next morning he went over to the front of the monastery on the other side of the valley. It was enclosed by a wall like that of a castle, and behind the door restless dogs were rattling their chains. In the broad courtyard a beech tree sheltered the well pulley. High facades with barred windows rose up on all sides, and in the rear, beside the chapel entrance, a guardian was reading his breviary on a stone bench.

When he saw Christopher he closed his breviary and examined him again, feeling a sense of satisfaction over his great and useful limbs. Then he led him through a high, cool gallery to a cloister that enclosed a garden where sand pathways encircled flowerbeds. A fountain was singing in the center and the ground between the ivy-covered walls was paved with flagstones, like the floor of a church. There four friars, their habits hitched up, were playing at bowls. Farther along others were chatting in the sun, and under a bower the abbot was dozing, his hands crossed over his stomach.

When Christopher appeared, everything came to a halt and everybody raised their eyes as a rumor of wonderment ran all about. Then the guardian who was standing in front of Christopher, hesitant, made a sign for him to go over to the abbot.

His Reverence gave a start in his chair on finding himself face to face with the monster. Then he lifted his hands up to Heaven with a look of compassion. As a demonstration of Christopher's strength, the guardian had him pick up a pillar that was lying on the ground. Christopher brandished the pillar as though it were a simple shepherd's crook, and the monks all drew back with great "Ahs!" of amazement.

Christopher was taken on for work in the monastery, performing the tasks of many servants. But the cook asked if there were really any savings because at the same time he would consume the rations of many men. The friars discussed the concern with great gravity but the abbot decided the matter. In addition to the savings, the monastery would have the glory of having that strongest of men there. So Christopher was immediately taken to the stables to clean them out.

He was the serf of the monastery and upon him fell all the work of the community, which consisted of eighty friars, thirty novices, and numerous dependents. He swept the courtyards, curried the mules, cultivated the gardens, whitewashed the walls, carried sacks of flour, carted bundles of firewood, and was the one who brought large stones from the quarries for the work in the laundry. For long months his strong bones creaked under the heavy work. He would take the place of animals as he pulled heavy carts with iron axles. All day long, in the monastery or on the grounds surrounding it, in sunshine or rain, his strong figure went about in continuous labor. Only on occasions would he rest, drawing from the well a bucket of water that he would put to his lips and drain in one swallow. At night, lying on the flagstones in the courtyard, he would sleep the sleep of an animal among the loose dogs, who would place their paws on his chest as on the rim of a wall and bay at the sound of the night.

Every year on Candlemas eve, the teaching friar would gather the servants together and test them on doctrine. Christopher was unable to answer. He couldn't even recite the Lord's Prayer. He didn't know who had created the World and matters of Paradise were unknown to him. Aghast at such dark ignorance, the abbot ordered Christopher to attend the class in Sacred History. His immense body wouldn't fit in among the school benches, so the teaching friar arranged for Christopher to lean against the wall in the courtyard and put his head in through the open window of the classroom.

When the class bell rang, Christopher would go over to the wall and his great head of hair would rise up over the windowsill. All the students would laugh and the more daring would throw fruit pits at his face or tickle him with duck feathers, which would stick into his hair like small spears. He would smile, patient and respectful.

Sitting up on his dais, the teacher gave his lessons and Christopher, as through a fog, glimpsed the marvelous happenings of the beginning of the World. An enormous God, as huge as he, reached out his powerful arms and separated the Sun and the Moon. His voice was the roll of thunder and his breath made the forests bend over and the waves swell up. But men began to populate the Earth and God immediately flew into great rages. At his whim cities would crumble, burying under their ruins infants crying in their cradles, vast meadows dried up and cattle lowed lamentably from hunger as a great terror came over the Earth and men lived in great fear of the huge hand that came out of the clouds only to bring them devastation.

Come night, sweet sleep would abandon Christopher as he would lift his mistrustful eyes to the sky. What if God, catching sight of him, were suddenly to cast down the fire that had burned Gomorrah up? Any loud noise would upset him, and on one night of thunder his cries awoke the whole monastery.

But the teaching friar soon began to explain dogma, and it was as though all Heaven and Earth had lost their reality and all that was left of them were some low-floating clouds. On high, there no longer ruled a powerful old man with a long beard but a trinity, which was made up of three but which forms only one, and it was a Father, a Son, and a winged Spirit. Sin was not doing evil but just being born, and water poured from a shell washed it all away like a dirty rag. Christopher opened his eyes wide, and the preachments of the teaching friar were like clouds that floated out of reach and dissipated as soon as they were formed. He felt a kind of sadness about those inaccessible things, and the sigh that escaped his chest made the novices turn their heads and make devilish faces at him behind the priest's back.

Only one of them seemed to sympathize with Christopher. He was a delicate lad whose desk, over which his blond curls fell, was next to the window. His pale hands delicately turned the pages of his notebook and there was something about him that combined the seriousness of a scholar and the gentleness of a virgin.

Every day Christopher would watch him arrive from the village, his inkwell tucked in his belt and his roll of paper under his arm, and every afternoon his eyes would follow him when after class he would return to the village, still thumbing through some book with bright colors in it. Sometimes Christopher watched him stop to pick some wildflowers along the way. Or, as he let his long hair fall down across his back, the young hero would sing merrily in the gentleness of the afternoon.

Whenever he passed close to Christopher, he would say "God keep you!" to him, and it felt to Christopher something like a caress in his soul. Many were the times he thought about him, and he remembered what he had heard the teaching friar say about angels, who would come down to Earth and mingle in human affairs. Then he would go station himself along the road for when the boy would pass. And one day when the road was full of puddles, Christopher offered to carry him in his arms. Ever after that he looked for ways to be of service to him. On hot days he would have a pitcher of the coolest water for him and on cold days he would make a quick fire of branches in the courtyard where he could warm his feet before going up into the cloister. Finally, with winter coming on and afternoons growing darker, Christopher would follow him on his way back to the village to protect him from werewolves or from unpleasant encounters. And when the rains came he offered to carry him on his back like a mule to the door of his house. Then they would go along the way chatting in low voices as Christopher told him about his work at the monastery and the boy spoke about his wish to be a soldier, to know the world, and get to see its cities. His father was the land warden and had him destined for the priesthood, but the lad wanted to marry a cousin of his named Etelvina, who lived at the foot of the castle, beyond the Ladies' Pool. One day when they were chatting like that, the boy told Christopher that he would sometimes meet the girl farther off, by the edge of the woods, but he was afraid she would be surprised by his father's halberdiers or by castle serfs sent by Etelvina's father. If Christopher were willing, he could stay by the edge of the woods scouting the roads, just as from a watchtower, and if he saw someone coming he could advise them with a shout. Christopher said "I'll go wherever you want to send me."

viii/

The place where they would meet was in a clearing by the edge of the woods. In olden times there used to be a watchtower that the Count of Occitania had built there. The Devil knocked it down one day, and traces of the Tempter's claws could still be seen on the blackened stones. A feeling of fright kept human steps away from there, but the abundance of wildflowers and the soft mosses offered the brave souls who reached that place a cool refuge of sylvan peace. It was there that Alfredo and Etelvina would meet. For him to get there more quickly, Christopher would lift Alfredo up to his shoulders and with great steps the length of an ell, leaping over ravines and wading through marshes, he would be the first to arrive there in the cool of the evening. They would catch sight of Etelvina as she came down the road that curved around the hill, lifting the skirt of her gray dress because of the thorns on the hedges. As she was coming from church, she carried a book in her hand. Her two blond braids fell down over her shoulders. The long lashes of her lowered eyes cast a shadow over her face, which had the color and the softness of a white rose. And alongside her there was jangle of shears, keys, and a thimble as they hung from her waist by silver chains. The good student knelt before her, taking her delicate hand in his and walking with her through the woods, pausing to remove the brambles that were catching onto the hem of her skirt. She always had a smile for Christopher, one that matched the glow of her eyes, and as he stood there keeping watch down the road he thought about those eyes, which were stars for him. Birds were singing in the trees all about, and a smell of verdure, pines, and honeysuckle floated in the air. Sometimes a doe would brush against the tightly clumped young beeches and Christopher, as he leaned on his shepherd's crook, would cast his eyes all about the valley, but no one was approaching the tumbledown tower. And as he was slowly taken by the gentle afternoon, his thoughts turned to the gentle caresses of his mother's hands as they stroked his curly hair, and he thought about the frolics of children as they fearlessly climbed up onto his knees. A feeling of melancholy would then overtake his breast, and he wanted to enfold that entire valley with that vague, tender feeling, along with the clouds in the sky and the water that went singing as it flowed along.

In the meantime Alfredo and his beloved were taking their repose sitting on a rock. He would gaze at the hem of her dress or would grasp her delicate fingers as they plucked the petals from a marigold, one by one. Sometimes he would gather a bouquet or, picking up the book that had fallen by her feet, turn the pages. She would lie down and her loose tresses would brush against Alfredo's shoulders. They would often play that way, their eyes on the same page, not turning it, blushing and with their breasts heaving.

One day then, as they strolled off together for quite some time, deep into the pine grove, shoulder to shoulder, Christopher ventured to touch the book they had left lying on the rock, and with his thick fingers he turned the pages. There were black lines he couldn't understand, but he was taken with emotion when he saw the brightly colored pictures. It seems to have been a story, and it began with a small child in a pen between a cow and a donkey. He was smiling, his hair adorned with stars, as he sat on the knee of a pale woman. Then that same child, older now but still crowned with stars, was speaking before a group of bearded old men, who were clapping their hands in astonishment. Who was he, so young, to astonish those wise old men? Further on, as Christopher's fingers turned the stiff pages he came across that same person, whom he recognized from his circle of stars, a man now and wearing a tunic as he strolled along the shore of a lake. And he kept on appearing, laying his hands on cripples, reaching his arms out to children, unwinding the bandages of dead people, consoling the multitudes of crowds. Mounted on a donkey, he was passing through the gates of a city in the midst of a crowd acclaiming him by waving palm fronds. Sitting under a sycamore tree he listened to two women who were spinning by his feet. Then kneeling among olive trees, he was preaching on the top of a hill. A prisoner now surrounded by soldiers carrying torches, he was appearing before a judge who was holding up a finger and pondering.

And Christopher, when he saw the two lovers before him, their arms locked and smiling, felt a great longing to understand. Surprised, Christopher closed the book. And when Etelvina saw how troubled his wide face was, she became filled with pity and she asked him if he loved the Lord. Christopher shook his head, not understanding. How could it be, then, that he didn't love the Lord and didn't love his gentle ways? Such great ignorance in that soul filled her with piety, and a scruple made her cheeks flush as she thought that while she had been busy thinking about her love, somebody right there before her was living without any knowledge of the Lord. Then, so that they would be worthy of Jesus and as payment for Christopher's protection, she asked Alfredo that they read the holy book to that simple man, who was ignorant of it.

It was the next day, on an autumnal afternoon. The trees were starting to lose their leaves and the brook sang more sadly under a sky bathed in paleness. In order to hear better, Christopher had seated himself on a pile of fallen rocks. Alfredo, smiling, had climbed onto his broad knee and Etelvina had sat down on the other, as though it were nothing but a rock or a grassy mound. Her small feet were crossed, like those of an angel, and her hands rested modestly in her lap. Facing her, Alfredo opened the book and with Christopher's wide face between them, it looked as though they were sitting on the cold hard limbs of an enormous stone statue.

So all afternoon, in the silence of the grove, Alfredo read about the life of the Lord. He spoke of the star that shone over his crib and the shepherds who came to him from far away, along with the kings who were bringing him treasures. Then hard-hearted men appeared, bearing scimitars. Then the child was smiling, asleep at his mother's breast as the donkey carried them off to Egypt with brisk steps. There they rested under a palm tree as the child laughed and tugged at the beard of his father whose crook burst into bloom like the stalk of a lily. But it was time for Saint Anne, holding a long scroll on her knees, to teach the Child to read. His father was smiling behind his great beard. Little Saint John, at his side, was listening, his hands underneath his chin. And two angels, on high, raised their hands to halt the breezes so there would be no sound to disturb the Child as he learned. The Child learned quickly, because surprise at his wisdom showed in the eyes of the bearded elders in their miters . . .

Weary of reading, Alfredo stopped, his finger between the pages of the book. And Christopher's simple face showed the same surprise as was evident on the faces of the doctors. His thick lips trembled and he whispered humbly, full of love now:

"And what did the Child do?"

Who knows? A soft silence fell over the land. In Nazareth the carpenter is planing his board and Saint John, his hair loose in the wind, is leaving for the desert. In the distance, now, the clear waters of a lake are gleaming. Boats are beached on the sand. Jesus is speaking slowly, lifting up his arms, and the fishermen abandon their nets, sowers leave off their seeding, tax collectors leave their posts, and the poor come away from the street corners as Jesus sets off on his walk to Judaea, and incomparable delight fills the life of these men. Jesus is among them. Those who had been unable to see acclaim the splendor of the light, those who'd been unable to walk are running up and down the hills singing. All their demons have vanished. The dead untie their winding cloths. There is no sorrow without hope of consolation. Children have a friend and the crowds in the villages watch bread being born from bread.

Why is he going to Jerusalem, a harsh land, where men with pointed beards are shouting at each other and brandishing scrolls that contain the Law? But it matters not! He will make men better and the people go along with him, singing. Then the sky begins to darken. The Pharisees are plotting under the archways of the Temple and anxiety weighs down over the land . . .

And an anxiety fills the face of Christopher. Why hadn't Jesus always stayed a Child on his mother's knee while the Star shined and he reached out his little hand to stroke the muzzle of the cow? Or, if he was to be a man, why did he leave the shore of the lake for the green pathways where, with every step of his, the earth grew better, as did the souls of men as well?

"Are you sad, Christopher?"

It was Etelvina who whispered that, with a pity showing in her eyes.

He nodded silently. His broad chest was heaving and a terror was coming over him as he looked upon the one who was so good in that city where men were so harsh.

"And then?"

Alfredo then spoke of the final days. Jesus, sad and all alone, at evening tide, went up to the garden of Bethany. There came the melancholy of a happiness that is approaching its end. Magdalen, her hair loose, is washing his tired feet. Martha is sewing, ever so slowly, as though she were sewing a winding cloth. And now Jesus is sitting down to the Last Supper. Saint John rests his head on the Master's breast. Under his tunic Judas is clutching his black purse. Jesus is saying, "Soon I shall not be among you." The night is dark. Jesus slowly goes up the hill where there are olive trees, and an angel, all in black, floats along in the air beside him. A breeze passes through the branches of the olive trees. The sound of weapons comes along with the passage of the wind . . .

Great tears well up in Christopher's eyes and Alfredo tells of torches rising through the darkness of the branches, the brutal soldiers, and the Lord's imprisonment. Why did they arrest him and drag him through the streets like that, he who was sweeter and gentler than a lamb? Behold the one who passes! His feet, which mark the way of the good, tread the hard stones leading from the house of Pilate to the house of Caiaphas. His face carries blood on it, his hands are red and swollen from the cord that binds him, his shoulders crisscrossed with the marks of the rod that has struck him. And yet his gentleness is so great that he says, "Why do you beat me?" The cross that they give him, he with great beads of sweat on his face, is so heavy that it falls to the ground, once, then again . . . He injures his knees on the stones. . . . And behold how in confusion they all climb the hill. They pound great nails through his hands and into the wood, they drive great nails through his feet into the wooden cross. . . . And, though no one hears him, he pleads, to quell his thirst, for a sip of the water he had used to slake the thirst of the multitudes. Evil men hurl rocks at him and his cross. And every form of Evil is done. To him who had done nothing but Good!

And then a great sigh shook Christopher's breast, and, in the solitude of the forest, he cried out, "Oh, why was I not there with my strong arms?"

The two well-loved ones were standing in front of him, and the enormous man was sobbing. He sobbed for the death of him whom he'd come to know so late. He sobbed for all those who, with his death, would lose mankind's greatest friend. But why did they kill him . . . ? Why did they kill him? And Christopher, taking leave of the two, went back down the hill, sobbing.

Night was falling on the valley. A sad wind bent over the cane fields. Christopher continued on, still sobbing. His huge feet knocked the rocks aside as if they were pebbles. His shoulders, as they surged forward, broke the tender boughs. Oh, if only he'd been there on that dark hilltop when they arrested him! His arm would have plucked him away, as one does with dried herbs, from the glistening swords. He'd have put the adored Master over his shoulder. He'd have fled with him to the peace of the fields; and, like the loyal dog that follows your every step, he'd have defended that body that was of God from the soldiers and the priests, and he'd have sown the seeds of God among men.

Now that night had fallen, Christopher stopped. And seated on a rock, with great tears covering his face, he looked up at the stars which, one by one, marked the points of Heaven. It was there, in those realms, that Jesus resided. Oh, if only he could ascend there and see what his face was like, and feel the softness of his hands! Why would he never again return to console the poor, to dry their tears, to bundle up the little children, and to feed the multitudes? Now, when all loved him, no one would arrest him. The path that he followed would be strewn with roses; the bishops, in their capes of gold, singing and carrying the censers, would come to his gatherings. And to defend him the barons, covered in iron, bearing lances, and astride their chargers would come running. Why would he not return? He, Christopher, would follow his light, blessed steps throughout the world. At every step, he would clear away the rude thorns and brush so that they didn't tear and bruise him; with great cries he would frighten away the dogs that bark at the doors of the castles; whatever burdens there were, he would bear them happily; only he, and no one else, would gather fruit for the Lord, or would go to fetch water at the best springs. At night, he would build a shelter with tree boughs to protect him from the harsh wind. And he would stretch out his arm for him, so that he could lay down his weary head. And, thinking these thoughts, an immense love surged up in Christopher's breast, and, standing up now on a rock, he raised his arms to the heavens in order to embrace, through them, him who for the salvation of mankind had been nailed to the cross. And three times he cried out, "Jesus, Jesus, Jesus!"

Then, as if next to him, he heard a weeping-like sound that was cutting through the silence of the night. It was coming from some distance away, where a light inside a hovel was shining. Crushing the fresh ground underneath them, his steps took him toward that place. And as he got closer, he recognized the sound of a woman sobbing. Certainly, someone was suffering a great deal. An orphan or a widow must be there, or some misery that was lifting its arms upward toward Heaven. Why would the Lord not come to help? If he inhabited the earth, it was to that hut that his steps would be coming. He, Christopher, would humbly walk behind, following him. But Jesus was up there, behind those stars. Why could he not go there, too, as if following the Lord? More poignant now, and sadder, the weeping cut through the night. And Christopher, slowly and fearfully, knocked on the door of the hut.

ix /

Long days have now passed, and Christopher, in the village, is everyone's servant. The doors of the monastery are no longer closed, because there peace and abundance reside. The granaries are full of wheat, the cellars full of wine, and a great happiness and pride reign supreme in hearts. And there it was certain that the steps of Jesus would not go, as Christopher's would not, because he followed his Lord. But in the village there were old people, beggars, the sad, the orphaned, the widowed. And the strength of Christopher's arms belongs to them, as does the love of his heart, because that was how his Lord would have it.

Simple and timid, Christopher offers them his service. But until that point, weakness, which had always had recourse to his strength, now wins the gratitude of his soul. And little by little, sensing in him someone who would help them, all of the weak came to him, so that from the moment the morning star appears until night covers the valley, Christopher now works with such happiness that the weight of the greatest burdens seems to him a caress and from the healing of the worst wounds he senses an ineffable perfume. He ploughs the fields of the old people, he hews the forests with great blows of his ax, he drains the swamps with great pipes that he has hauled there on his back, he pulls the carts so the oxen don't become exhausted, he rocks the cradles, he digs the graves of the deceased, and when there's no wind he, bracing his arm muscles, makes the mill's grinding stone turn round and round. His name is constantly shouted back and forth over the fences by the people who live there. This one has a sick donkey, and it's Christopher who carries its burdens; that one needs a harvester, and it's Christopher who heads out with a scythe. That roof needs some thatching, and it's Christopher who carries up the material by the armload. There are no rocks nearby to build the widow's house, and it's Christopher who, returning from a faraway quarry, groans under the weight of the great blocks of stone he carries back. It's Christopher who blows on the blacksmith's fire, it's Christopher who, in the mornings, pulls the bell-tower rope. It's he who, all alone and laboring in the mud, puts the new walkways in. It's he who digs the new wells in the yards of the houses. At night, he was prostrate with exhaustion. When the winter rains would flood the village, he would seek shelter under a vast porch that scarcely covered him. In the summer, he would stretch himself out next to the cross and the first little birds of the day, chirping in the light of dawn, would alight on his shoulders, as if on dark hilltops.

On Sundays, he would rest, and that was his best day because the little children would play with him. Finding Christopher to be sweet and patient, they would all run to him as they would a big animal that was entertaining to them. And climbing up on him was like the thrill of climbing trees and towers. Sometimes, with his hands resting on the earth, he would offer them his broad back so that, holding on tightly to his sash and forming a line of agile and lively little bodies, they could ride him horseback. And then, bucking, he would imitate, amongst delighted laughing and giggling, the roar of a lion or the heroic whinny of a great courser. In addition to this, he knew how to use his hands, hairy and covered with earth, to make all sorts of toys — hunting arrows, small carts that rolled through the dust, and sailing ships that could navigate the deepest parts of the ocean. In him, the children had someone who was ready for everything — and he only recused himself when they were threatening to harm the green fruit or do ill to the orioles that were all about.

But of all the village's children, one governed his heart more than any other. She was the daughter of a widow, the one whom Christopher, as if sent by Jesus, his master, had heard crying and the one at whose door he had knocked. Her husband had died that same night, and the poor woman had no one left in the world, no one to tend the fields and care for the sheep. But, from that night on, a great and useful force had entered their hut. Christopher was their faithful servant. And no vegetable garden in the entire village was better watered, no cattle were pastured in better meadows, no earth more deeply plowed. A peal of laughter from the little girl (whose name was Joana) as she practiced her trick of pulling his beard, repaid him for all his labors. Even when he was playing with the other children, it was Joana he thought of. At night, he would pass by the door of the hut and listen to make sure she wasn't crying in her crib. And early in the mornings, he would station himself in the vegetable garden, between the lemon trees, in the hope that she would come running to him with her little arms wide open. And that all day long he would feel, in his hair and in his beard, the softness of her little hands, which tugged at him. He loved her with all his heart and being — the dimple on her face when she laughed, the grace of her still hesitant voice, and how her little feet stumbled over the ploughed ground. He especially loved her for her frailty — and he could envision no better life than to spend it eternally serving her, and being happily tugged on. His greatest pleasure was in carrying her astride his shoulders; she would laugh, clinging to his long hair, and he would walk along, grave and proud, as if he were part of the Sacred Host ceremony.

Sometimes, Christopher would compare her to the Child, to the divine Child, who would laugh in his manger and who would learn to read from the great book of Saint Anne. His clear, wide eyes must be like those of Joana. And Christopher's only regret was not knowing how to read, so that, resting it on his knees, he could open a book and let her little fingers move along following the large letters. Certainly Jesus, if he knew her, would have to love her. She was so innocent, like a flower from the valley floor. And her guardian angel would wait quietly when she would stop along the road to poke around in the dirt looking for bugs. No matter how far away his work took him, he heard Joana's voice if it called to him. He heard it as if it were coming from above, from Heaven, and he would hurry his work along, straining his mighty arms so he could run to her, but not forgetting to bring her some of the mulberries she liked, or, less rosy than her little face, some strawberry tree blooms. As friends, then, they would spend hours together, and Christopher was so simple that, to entertain her, he only knew how to imitate the sounds of the animals and to dance, heavily, like a bear.

Her mother would then say, "Christopher, Christopher, you're spending a lot of time with the little girl. . . . Mind the firewood, mind the cattle. . . ."

He would lower his head, open the gate, and go . . . even as he would later return from afar smiling and with his vast face shining.

Now it happens that in the midst of all this happiness, malicious mutterings began to be heard in the village. The monastery guardian had not pardoned Christopher for having abandoned his duties to the order.

And the monks who would pass by, or those who came in the afternoons to pray in the churchyard, would later say that, according to their books, all giants had pacts with Satan. This one, certainly, was sweet and obliging in his duties. But that was how those giants were whose arts served the Devil, who, for some time, had been making them sweet and affable, the better to overpower their souls and take control. The women, upon hearing this, became pensive. It was then May, when the crab apple trees were flowering, when the first sprouts of wheat were poking up from out of the earth, and when the meadows were turning green. But it came to pass, one night, that great flashes of lightning lit up the valley, thunder rumbled over the mountains — and suddenly, like the crash of lances clanging against each other, the hail began to fall. It fell for a long time, ruining the thatched roofs of the huts, killing the newly born lambs, smashing the fruit, and devastating the cattle in the pens. By morning, the entire village was impoverished. And the men hurried through the fields, checking out the destruction, while the women, gathered together in the churchyard, wailed as if at a funeral. An elderly padre came quickly from the monastery and, extending his hand, indicated that, because of the hardening of the souls there, that terrible visitation had come. Why did they persist in being friendly with a servant of the Devil? Christopher, like all giants, was an emissary of Beelzebub. You could see Hell itself in his eyes, in the fires that had singed his beard and in his feigned humility. But they continued to give him his daily bread and salt, and that was why the Lord had devastated their sown fields and flocks. All afternoon he spoke like that, while Christopher was working in the fields, tying up the fallen limbs, draining the puddles, and fixing the roofs of the huts.

The men, in the meantime, took up their shepherd's crooks. The bailiff who'd been summoned, blew his bugle in order to assemble the halberdiers. Some of the women hid their children while others planted crosses in front of the doors to their homes. The abbot ordered that the church bell be rung. And it was all like what happened when a band of wolves would appear in the village.

Christopher would likely come home along a particular country lane, and so it was there that the men posted themselves, with their crooks, the halberdiers with their crossbows cocked and ready, and with the padre, behind them, lifting high, with a trembling hand, his cross. And in another group, the women of the village, even the old, unsteady ones, wanted to see the false prophet beaten and expelled. Everyone there had received Christopher's help; for every one of them, he'd dug the ground, transported their goods, split the wood, and trimmed the cattle. But now, in each one of those services, they saw him as a sly and clever Satan. A thousand things they remembered, all of which now condemned him. One night there had appeared a disinterred old man. Who would have disinterred him if not Christopher? Sometimes, at night, there shone in the darkness covering the village two huge red eyes. Who would they be from, if not Satan, who'd come along in the dead of night to converse with Christopher? Why did he never pray in the churchyard? Others agreed, affirming that he had painted, on his back, a skull. And that was certainly the seal of Death. Some who remained doubtful about all this were fearful of defending him in order that they not seem, in front of the monks, to be inclined toward the Enemy. And thus it was that they were waiting for him when, trudging along the path that led down from the mountain range, Christopher finally appeared, bent over under the immense weight of a bunch of broken branches and boughs. The padre immediately raised high the crucifix, and the halberdiers pulled tight their bows — and from the people a clamor arose, while men and women also bent over to pick up big stones.

Frightened, Christopher stopped. And so certain was he of having everyone's love that he turned around to see what terrible enemy or fearful man was coming down the path behind him and that had awakened the rancor of the village. But the path, now dark, was empty. And he saw that it was against him that the monk raised his cross, that the foolish people pointed their darts at him, and that those fists trembled with anger in the air!

"Vade retro! Vade retro!," shouted the monk.

"To the crows! To the crows, Evil One," clamored the multitude. Letting slip down from his shoulders his burden of branches and boughs, which struck the hedge, crushing it in the process, Christopher lifted up his face and extended his arms. Just for a moment, the fear he felt made his face so ugly that the mob moved back and the women fled from him, their arms stretching upward. But the monk, tremulously holding the crucifix in the air, was piling up the exorcisms, the bailiff incited the multitude with his staff—and the stones, hurled with such fear that some of them were lost in the surrounding forest, were launched. Then, without fear, Christopher took a slow step. His astonished eyes were taking in the blustering, bawling mob. He saw there, screaming at him, all of those whom he'd helped. The miller, whom he had served as a beast of burden and for whom he'd carried so many bundles, now brandished a crook at him; the widow of the blacksmith, whose forge he'd breathed air into, clutched two stones in her hands; and the children he had so cherished in the churchyard now shouted at him, "To the crows!" It was at that moment that Christopher felt a sharp pain pierce his simple heart. The village didn't love him any longer; it did not want him any more. Like a hungry animal, like a wolf, he was being chased away. Two tears clouded his vast, glistening pupils, and, lowering his head with great humility, Christopher headed back up the path. At that point, the multitude gained new rancor. The stones, flying freely now, struck him about the shoulders, which were weary from bearing so many burdens. An arrow got entangled in his shaggy hair. Christopher disappeared.

In front of him were the mountains, and it was toward the mountains that he slowly climbed. And only one doubt turned tumultuously in his heart: Why had they persecuted him? What had he done? He had loved them all and he'd served them all. Was it that his labors were not perceived to be useful enough? He could not extract any more strength from out of his muscles, nor could he make the days longer so that he could toil on even more. Why had they stoned him, then? And then a remembrance came into his soul, the memory of Jesus, who had also done only good and whom men had beaten and tormented as he was held prisoner against a stone column. He was, then, like the Lord, one who had been persecuted. And an even greater love for Jesus grew in his soul, and he felt, confusedly, that there was in their destinies an equality of suffering. . . . Christopher's arms stretched out toward the moon, which was just coming up. There, up in the heavens, was the Lord. And even seeing the moon so brilliant and yet so sad, he wondered if that could not be the face of the Lord!

Such were the thoughts running through his head as he sat there on a rock. The eyes of a wolf glowed from between the trees of the forest. He thought that the wolf was perhaps hungry and that it would go down into the village. Standing upright, he let out a fierce cry and frightened the wild beast back into the deep woods, far from the paths that led down to the village.

Christopher could see them, those pathways, in between the pine trees. And further down, he could see the dim lights from the houses, and further down still he could make out the Pego da Dona, shining like a silver disk. And there was the hut where, at that very hour, Joana was sleeping. Never again would he see her stretched out in her basket, covered with her mother's black blanket. Never again would her little hands tug at his beard. And an immense sadness overtook him, a desire to lie down forever there, on the ground of the mountain range, and to stay there until his white bones could not be distinguished from the white stones about them. But who would make Joana laugh, as he could, when his arms would lift her up as high as the highest bough of the pine trees? And who would work the widow's fields? She, certainly, would lament his departure from the village. In her, he had always found gentleness, and a countenance that always smiled in the face of his sadness. If she were to see him again, she would certainly say, "Christopher, mind the cattle; Christopher, mind the firewood!. . . ." If the others pursued him, she, at least, would take him in and give him shelter. And now Christopher awaited the dawn so he could head down to where Joana lived.

Faint and fresh, dawn finally broke over the mountains. Creeping along through the trees, crouching down so that his head wouldn't be seen over the shrubs and bushes, Christopher circled about before descending to the widow's hut. The gate was locked. The cock, on top of his roost, was crowing. The fire must have already been lit because smoke was coming out of the chimney over the top of the loosely tiled roof. Skylarks were busy singing high up in the clear air. Christopher appeared behind Joana's mother, who was standing in front of the yard door. A terrified cry cut the air. The widow saw Christopher and, snatching up Joana, who was playing on the floor, fled inside the hut, screaming, like the padre, *Abrenuntio!*

Christopher froze. So she, too, feared him and wanted him around no longer. There was not a single heart in the entire village who remembered him. Why? Slowly, his steps began to carry him away. He was so sad that the skylarks' song almost made him cry. Standing next to him, the Pego da Dona was shining more brightly than ever, like a round mirror. Bending over it, he looked at his face. It was then, and for the first time, that he felt his ugliness. He must have repelled the others, he thought, because of this monstrous visage. Christopher left forever the place he'd been born.

X

He walked for many long days. The country was a desert, full of great rocks and crags. His thirst carried him to a brook he'd found gurgling between some stones. He drank and then pressed on, following the clear water that was escaping from the ground. At the end of a long trek, he came across a river. Gentle hills, splashed with little white houses, rose up along the two sides of the mute, serene stream, lined with willows. An ancient bridge connected the two banks, and once across it, Christopher saw, rising up and scalloped out of the bright morning air, the walls of a city. Almost at the same moment, two doors, under a tower that rose up over the ramparts, swung open. And from out of these there burst a multitude of people in full flight. There were people carrying their sleeping pallets on their backs and jugs of water in their arms. There were children, crying and clinging to their mothers' skirts. There were old people, with their arms outstretched, beseeching the others not to leave them behind. And from time to time everyone would draw away from some knightlike horseman who, cloaked in his cape and with the feather in his cap waving in the wind, was trying to get away at a full gallop on his skinny jennet. A cloud of smoke, as if coming from many fires, was rising up from behind the walls. The battlements had no sentinels, and the air was full of the tolling of the tower bells for the dead and dying.

The fleeing mob, upon seeing Christopher, became even more frightened. Stumbling, people were falling down under the burden of their bundles. Christopher extended his arms to help the old people, but their terror only increased — and around his legs, as if around the great towers themselves, the stampeding, screaming people streamed.

Finally, he arrived at the entrance into the city. Two astonished soldiers slammed the doors shut. Christopher leaped across the moat and stepped over the walls. A street opened up in front of him, one littered with scraps and rags, and everywhere there were closed doors underneath their signboards, which were creaking on their iron rods in the fierce wind. A terrible, fetid stench made the air heavy, and two friars, lifting up their cassocks, were fleeing from a man who was writhing on the ground, his face completely green and his mouth open wide, crying for water! Christopher ran to him, lifted him up in his arms, and carried him to a fountain, where the water was gushing out of gargoyles. The man gulped down long droughts of water — and then his legs went stiff and, suddenly dead, he remained there, all but decomposed, on Christopher's knees. But then, from a nearby house, shouts erupted, and, lifting up his face, Christopher saw a disheveled old woman who, from a tall, narrow window, where, in a vase, stood the stalk of a dry flower, was wringing her hands and shouting for help. From the nearby windows other pale faces were peering out. Further away, new crying and sobbing could be heard. Christopher, having now laid the cadaver on the ground, was looking all around, distressed, and without understanding the nature of the pain that seemed to have befallen the city. Suddenly, from out of a tavern, some drunken soldiers appeared, staggering and stumbling, singing loudly, and with their faces livid from a night of wine and debauchery. Christopher was about to go over and question them when — suddenly — one fell to the ground, writhing in agony. The others, now sobered up, fled. And as Christopher was tending to the one who was in agony, he, too, went stiff and died. At the end of the street, a religious procession was passing by. A priest, wearing a white tunic, was holding on high a glinting reliquary while barefoot, unkempt women, following behind, were wrenching their arms and pleading for mercy from Heaven above. The bells did not cease their tolling for the dead, and men carrying kegs of tar set fires on the street corners, whose flames reached up into the air and caused the glass in the latticework windows to shatter.

On one corner, a baker, more pale than candle wax, opened up the wooden door of his shop. Christopher approached him and, bending down and placing his hands on his knees, asked him what evil had befallen the city and why was there such lamentation. The man stepped back, unsure, then asking, in his turn, if he, Christopher, had come with the acrobats, jugglers, and mountebanks to put on a show. Christopher said no, and with a gesture pointed to the distant horizon from which he'd come. Then the man advised him to flee, because the entire city was dying from the black plague.

As they were talking of these things, the sound of iron chains being dragged across the paving stones reverberated through the air. And two men, made prisoners by the leg irons on their feet, appeared bearing a dead man on a litter. Behind them were other men, with sinister faces and also wearing leg irons, bearing other dead people. . . . These were the galley slaves who were to bury the dead, and they were being guarded by soldiers who made the air crack with their long, leather whips. Christopher then placed on his shoulders the two dead men who were stretched out next to the fountain, and began to follow the galley slaves. Thus did they pass out from the gates until arriving at an olive tree grove, where a cross had been planted. An irregular and tortuous ditch zigzagged underneath the pale leafage. Working quickly, the slaves tossed the bodies into it and, with their hoes, covered them with a thin layer of dirt. Reacting to the noise, a flock of crows that had settled in the olive trees, took flight, cawing furiously.

Christopher shook the dirt off his hands and, paying no heed to the shouts of the soldiers who were calling to him, returned, aimlessly, to the city by a different gate, one entirely taken over by yet another funeral. Here, though, there were friars, shield-bearers, and pages bearing a casket with large candles on it and with a velvet shroud featuring an embroidered coat of arms. For the rest of the day, then, Christopher scoured the streets helping those who had fallen, clearing the dead away from the walkways, and, by nightfall, he'd become so familiar a figure to the people that, from the latticework windows, they would shout to him, "Hey, you!" And he would come, bearing their dead off to the ditch, cleaning up the filth and vermin from their yards, and running to fill their water jugs — even feeding the little children, who, all alone now, were crying in their hovels.

Since there was at least one death in every house, and since there was widespread fear of the contagion, the people, delirious and given over to alarm, roamed the streets in terror. The women and the old people, who were running to the churches to beseech the holy relics for assistance, leaped over the cadavers that were piling up in the churchyards. Other people, judging the world to be coming to an end, raced to the taverns and broke into the wine casks, and the blasphemies of the drunks joined with the wailing of the women. On every street corner there were brawls — and from time to time, on some deserted street whose residents had all died, Christopher had to drive away the pigs that were gnawing on human bones. Other abandoned animals also roamed the streets, and sometimes a frightened horse or a bull, now escaped from the slaughterhouse, ran loose, trampling people, and it was Christopher who had to secure them with his enormous fists.

At every instant, the cries of the sick people who'd been abandoned stopped him. Creeping along very carefully, he introduced his vast body into the narrow stairways and went to give water to the ill, to clean the filth from them, and to offer them his great breast so that they could die feeling the warmth of a human heart. Sometimes, a dying person wanted extreme unction, but the padres had fled, and the rare ones who remained were not enough to serve so many dying people. And Christopher, picking up a crucifix, would get down on his knees next to the fetid bed and say, "Jesus, my Lord, be with this poor soul!"

Every night there were scenes of great penitence. Bands of men and of semi-nude women would roam the streets, rending their flesh, covering their faces in mud, and singing ferocious canticles in which invocations to the Lord were confused with appeals to the Devil. From time to time, a voice would suddenly cry out, "It's the fault of the Jews!" And the mob, grabbing up cattle prods and torches, would run to the Jewish homes, whose men would appear offering them bags of gold. But they would be knocked down under a rain of blows or have their beards set afire.

On the wealthy streets, the palaces were closed. But through the windows, music could be heard, along with the tinkling of silverware, because some were thinking that one should await death in the lap of luxury. Others, however, were going from house to house in a series of endless revelries. And capeless cavaliers with drops of wine on their sharp beards were wandering the streets, amongst mandolin and flute players, and, in their pointed shoes, stumbling over the abandoned bodies. And so as to see them pass by, pale women emerged from the balconies, women with their breasts uncovered, with ermine furs on the borders of their garments, and their heads covered with the hats worn by those condemned by the Inquisition, and from which were hanging bunches of long ribbons that the breeze was causing to flutter, like pennants on a ship's mast.

Christopher had worked all night long. Since the guards did not always close the city's gates, sometimes the wolves, attracted by the smell of rotting flesh, would appear in the darkness. And Christopher, who was collecting the cadavers, would chase after them, shouting, and with a torch in his hand. He would gather together the dead bodies and, on the following morn, carry them to the olive tree grove where he would bury them. After that, he would go up into the mountains to collect the aromatic herbs that salved the infection. Positioning himself on the street corners, he would offer them to the people who'd left their dwelling places to come see what was happening and who, taking a handful of them, would then walk off breathing easier and with confidence. And since thieves were in great abundance, Christopher would stand vigilant over the houses of the money changers and the jewelers, and if he surprised any men running away who seemed to be concealing something under their tunics, he would take it away from them and deposit it in a church. It was he, Christopher, who distributed the water, who swept away the vermin and filth, and who lit the fires that cleansed the air. And little by little he became so familiar a figure that the women, seeing his shadow pass close by their latticework windows, would call down upon him the blessings of the Lord. The rich would toss him bags of gold with which he would buy bread for the widows. Christopher's steps were sometimes hindered by the children, who swarmed around his legs as if they were great columns. Merchants opened up their tents to him. When he would kneel down at the door of some church, the prayers inside became even more ardent. And because he hauled the soldiers' firewood, polished their arms, and checked on them during his rounds — the soldiers in the streets would shout to him, "Viva Christopher!"

This great popularity disquieted the prince's nephew, who — since his uncle had fled the plague with his treasure and concubines — was now governing the city and who wanted, thanks to his ambition and his thirst for power, to win the sympathies of the people. But his livid, hard face, set atop a dwarfish and hunchbacked body, not only displeased the women because of its ugly mien but also the soldiers, who were suspicious of his weakness and defects. One day, as the nephew was following a procession bearing the relics of Saint Teódulo, the people, as he passed by, scarcely bent their knees in homage. Only a little further behind, however, and amongst the people, came Christopher, who was like a great tower among hovels and huts. A rich merchant had given him twenty bolts of linen cloth from Flanders for a new frock, and Christopher, waving about the two green palm fronds the members of the Brotherhood of Charity had given him as an emblem of his act of kindness, smiled in his simplicity. Upon seeing him, the people, who were thronging against the closed doors along the way, began, while heaping blessings upon him, to shout out his name: "Christopher the good! Christopher who pleases God!" One lady tossed him a flower that she'd been carrying in her bosom. The old people lowered their heads to him, as if honoring the passage of a righteous man.

The count, up ahead, became more pale than normal. And that night, as he sat by his great hearth and loosened his doublet, he muttered "Who will free me from that monster who has so transfixed the people?" The guards, having joined together in a corner and animated by their adulation of the count and his secret wish, came running and gathered around his high-backed chair. It was not, in truth, proper, in his mind, that such a disfigured being, one of those creatures one sees at the fairs, could win the affections of the people. . . . Besides, his great strength could easily be overcome with heavy iron chains. And was there not, outside of the city, some craggy precipice from which one could throw the body of the immense brute? And so, the next morning, when Christopher began to partake of his meal alongside the cathedral, a smiling page came by and invited him to a meeting with the prince, who, he said, wanted to give him the gold and garments that were appropriate for a man who served his people in such illustrious ways. Thinking that the clothing could serve to cover the galley prisoners, whom misery had rendered naked, Christopher shook out his hands, which had just broken his cornbread, and obeyed the page, who had to run to stay ahead of his giant steps.

Christopher had scarcely entered the palace when the thick, iron reinforced doors were slammed shut behind him. The count, who was up on a balcony and waving his plumed cap, shouted at him: "Well, well, Christopher!" And just as the latter, smiling and looking up, took a step toward the balcony, from which a gold-trimmed velvet cloth hung down, two soldiers rudely thrust a wooden beam between his legs and Christopher tumbled to the ground. Immediately, and from out of all the doors, innumerable men came running and, like ants covering a tree trunk, climbed all over Christopher's immense, prostrate body. In an instant, he was bound up with thick iron chains. And so that no cry for help could pass his lips, a gag was placed over his mouth. Then, stepping back quickly, everyone stared in silence at the conquered giant. In order to view him better, the prince, accompanied by his ladies, whose gown trains were like long sections of carpet sliding over the courtyard floor, descended the balcony staircase. The pages spat on his bearded face. Christopher thought of the Lord and how he, too, had been tormented — and then, and even more, he thought about the poor people he'd served and who, that day, would certainly miss him. All day long, he remained in that condition, surrounded by lackeys and by the kitchen help, who had abandoned their labors in order to come see him — and in some of whose hearts there would surely be at least a morsel of compassion.

Night descended, starless and dark. It was then that Christopher opened his eyes. The palace mastiffs, running loose, patrolled the courtyard. The sentinel was sleeping, and he and his lance were leaning up against the door. From up in the palace's high, pointed archways there came a clarion call and then the rumor of violins. At that moment, Christopher flexed his great muscles and with a great crash all of the chains broke apart. In the face of the gigantic form that was rising up in front of them, the huge dogs fled, barking in fear. The sentinel, grabbing his lance, also fled. With a single blow of his shoulder, Christopher broke through the door, leaped over the moat, and headed out into the deserted streets of the city. But suddenly he stopped, thinking that, if he revealed the count's treasonous conduct, the people and the soldiers would not love him for doing so; indeed, they would seek to do him ill. But if he were silent about it, the count would certainly order him killed. Perplexed, this is how he remained for a time; either his own blood would be made to run by others, or his blood would run by his own doing. Then, Christopher set out toward the great gate of the city. In the light of a retable in honor of the Virgin, some soldiers were shooting dice. And seeing Christopher, they asked him if the prince had given him some kind of reward or cloth for new clothes. Christopher murmured, "The prince gave me more than I expected." And then he continued on, penetrating the dark and heading down the road that led away, and leaving forever the city where he had been good to the afflicted.

xi/

For many long days Christopher wandered the roadways, until one afternoon he arrived at the foot of a mountain, whose rocks the setting sun was covering in rose-colored light. A man, wearing a friar's cassock with a long hood out from under which a white beard protruded, was slowly ascending a steep ravine. He was groaning under the load of firewood he bore. The friar, fearing a demon, made the sign of the cross in the air, and, since Christopher made the same sign on his chest, the friar then consented to allow him to lift the burden of firewood from his shoulders. And, wiping off the sweat with a ragged sleeve of his habit as he walked along at Christopher's side, the friar asked him if he had run away from the men who were exhibiting him at fairs. And since Christopher said that he'd come from the city, from far off, the friar understood that he'd most certainly appeared there because he was attracted to the saintliness of that mountain, peopled only by religious hermits. But to himself the friar also thought this: "Here is a man, certainly a simple one and one of immense strength, who could alleviate the burdens of the saintly men who live here, allowing them more time to perfect their souls and to give sure battle to the great Tempter. . . ."

He then took to guiding Christopher until they arrived at a rustic hut made from tree branches wedged between steep rocks. At the door of the shack, and firmly planted between two large stones, there stood a rough cross, and at its base, under a skull, there reposed an open notebook. Inside the hut there was only a bed made of dry leaves and a water pitcher with a broken handle.

The hermit, having indicated to Christopher where he was to put down his firewood bundle, took a horn that was hanging on the hut's door, and, clearing away the long hairs of his white moustache, blew three raucous calls, which echoed throughout the gorges. Timid and simple, Christopher considered each movement of the hermit to be like the actions of a saint.

Then, from the various mountain paths, there began to appear, walking slowly, some helped along by staffs and others with their hands hidden under their sleeves, a number of different hermits, all of whose faces were covered by long hoods. The first to arrive, coming up to Christopher, made the sign of the cross and then, with a gesture, signaled to the others, who, having been urged now to hurry along, began to leap from rock to rock. Almost all of them had long beards, greyish and unkempt, and tattered tunics, and the mud from the pathways was dry and crusty on their legs. With slow movements, they scratched their bodies, which itched from the vermin that covered them. And, if their legs or arms had wounds on them, they pulled up their tunics to show them off, as if taking pleasure from those miseries of the flesh. Some hermits, however, were new, and still robust, but already so pale that their faces, underneath their hoods, were like wax in the shadows. All of them bowed out of respect for the friar who'd guided Christopher there, and then they became more close-mouthed and mute than the images above a tomb. But at that point the hermit who seemed to have the authority of a prior explained that, at the foot of the mountain and coming back from gathering up firewood, he had met this man of such immense body and immense strength but so simple that he did not know where he'd come from or in what land he'd been born. And only later, like an inspiration coming from above, had the idea occurred to him to gather him in and to occupy him in the service of the saintly brothers who inhabited the mountain, in the manner of what Saint Antão had practiced in Egypt, where, in order that his wilderness brethren, and himself, better absorb themselves in prayer, and so that they might become freer to combat the Devil, he had taken on a very strong black man who could haul their water, split their firewood, secure the mules of the pilgrims, and transport the boxes and bags containing their provisions. Thus it was that, from that time forth, the hermits had someone who would serve them, so that their souls would not have to be bothered with anything except their conquest of Heaven. Having finished their business, and burying their faces even further under their hoods, as if deep in prayer, the hermits, without breaking their muteness, retraced the paths they'd come down the mountain on and, one by one, they all disappeared among the rocks and oak trees.

Alone, now, with Christopher, the hermit, returning to his hut, brought back a big piece of cornbread, a part of which he gave to Christopher. Both drank from the water jug. And, once he'd ordered Christopher, who was now carrying the wood on his shoulders, to take it up into the mountains and distribute it to the distant hermits who lived there, he stretched out in front of the cross and, laying his head on a rock, became immersed in prayer.

Christopher departed. Without speaking but using a slow hand gesture, each hermit would instruct him as to where the nearest chapel was. At all of them, there was the same bleached white skull next to the same cross. And at that particular time of the afternoon, the hermits were all gathered at the door of the chapel breaking bread together, pausing, from time to time, to take up either the books they were reading, the rosaries they were scrupulously reciting, some basket they were plaiting, or the mats they were weaving. From the door of each hut there hung a horn and a discipline whip, which was used for self-mortification and which had iron-tipped lashes. When Christopher would arrive, they would all direct their gazes downward. In some, the gaze was serene, albeit a dead kind of serenity. In others, it was like a cry of some kind of vague terror, or a light that seemed to extend itself outward in a kind of endless curiosity. Humbly, and with great respect, Christopher would lay down his load of firewood next to the altar. And the monks, watching his every movement, would once again hide their faces under the capes of their robes. When Christopher returned to the prior's rustic little chapel, he found him still stretched out, his head resting on a rock, and emitting sighs. Then, keeping very quiet, Christopher went over to a rock some distance away and sat down.

The sun, red like a mulberry, was setting in the distance. There was no sound to disturb the air. The world of men seemed to be very far away, and after those days spent in the plague city, Christopher felt that same serenity enter into his soul like a caress without end. But then he remembered those whom he'd left there, and he seemed even to see them in detail — the house on the corner where he'd brought bread to give to the abandoned children or the old man for whom he had gone to get the jug of water. He was missing those poor souls whom he had helped, but among these hermits there was such want and such need that it would certainly be sweeter still to occupy himself in their service. The sun had now disappeared. The valley of rocks was entirely covered in darkness.

From time to time, a great, dark bird would dive and swoop overhead. A tiny star sparkled, then another. The saintly prior was praying, with his face pressed up against the cold stone. And Christopher, now tired, stretched out his immense body on the earth and went to sleep.

Later, deep into the night, he awoke. The slow, desolate sound of a horn was resounding from rock to rock in the silence of the mountains. It was like the call of an afflicted heart. And immediately the prior came running out of his hut and fell on his knees in front of the cross, praying frantically. It had to be a far-off brother who was suffering a temptation from the Enemy, and who, already half defeated, was blowing his horn to tell the other hermits to help him with their prayers to reject Beelzebub. Sitting on his rocky crag, Christopher watched, full of simplicity, without understanding, and with his hands on his knees, as, from the other side of the range, and up high, another horn sounded, calling out help to another assailed soul. The prayers of the anchorite became even more frantic. But the horn's call grew still more distressed! And then the saintly man shouted to Christopher that he light a fire close to the cross so that, standing out in the dark against the red glow of the firelight, it would be seen by the demons who, on this particular night, seemed to be launching a terrible attack on the saintly mountain.

Knocking two rocks together to get sparks, Christopher, blowing on the embers, quickly made a fire. The new firewood crackled and popped and then a flame appeared, followed quickly by others that lit up the blackness of the night. And the sounds of the horns began to subside, like the anxieties of a heart calming down. A great silence then weighed on the evening and Christopher allowed his eyelids to close. And, for a moment, the prior warmed his trembling hands next to the flames.

But his eyes were fixed on the flames with a growing avidity. A flash of greed illuminated his face and his tongue appeared along the edge of his dry mouth, as if anticipating a big piece of succulent red meat, sizzling in the pan in which it had been roasted.... He'd even reached out, his hand open, to touch it. But then he cried out. How could he have let himself be so carried away that he didn't recognize an illusion of the Enemy when he saw it and how could he have allowed himself to be carried away by the temptation of gluttony?! Furious, he ordered Christopher to put the fire out.

With his arms crossed, the prior walked into the narrow strip of land bordered by large stones. As if he were chewing, his dry mouth was making a continuous noise, and he was stammering out prayers. Christopher's eyes, fixed on the live coals that were all that was left over from the fire, were beginning to close. All had become quiet on the mountain. And then, as if unconsciously attracted to it, the hermit gazed once again at the heap of glowing coals, which seemed to be fusing into a single red ember. What he now saw were mountains of money, ducats of gold, and mountains of scarlet rubies . . . an infinite glittering of treasures that then crumbled into dust. All he had to do was stretch out his hands and he would have treasure enough to buy an earldom, to erect great cathedrals, to hire mercenaries, to buy precious jewels for queens, and to have all the satisfactions of power and of love and of ecclesiastical vanity. And yet the hermit smiled, pulling on his long, white beard and murmuring, "I see well your illusion, oh Cursed One, you who judged me to be unprepared! But my soul is still strong, and in it, as the halberdier is in the tower, the power of prayer remains, full of strength . . . !" And with his foot, he scattered the hot coals. And Christopher thought, in his simplicity, "How many things this man sees that I do not see! It must certainly be because of his wisdom and his saintliness."

In the meantime, the hermit had returned to his hut. But, having scarcely gone into it, he let out a shriek and came running out, with his arms flung open wide, as if he'd witnessed some kind of vision. And he had. It was of a woman, splendidly white in color and totally nude, that he'd found stretched out on her back on his rude bed of branches and with her arms wide open, waiting for him and calling to him. And just for a second, his hands, as if impelled by some occult force, had reached out, irresistibly, for her. But at the last second, on her ever so white feet, he'd recognized a cloven hoof — and at that moment, as he blessed himself frantically, the woman evaporated, like a puff of black smoke does among the boughs surrounding his hovel. But he'd almost given in to this fearful illusion — and if, at the instant he'd reached out, he had died, eternal hellfire would have been his fate, complete and utter damnation! Violently, the hermit then grabbed his discipline whip and, tearing off his tunic, cried out, loudly, "My punishment, my holy punishment!" The hard strands of ox leather, with their iron tips, enveloped him down to the waist, tearing at the skin of his back. At each blow, he gave out a hoarse moan, but then, little by little, the moans changed from cruel and afflicted to low and languid, and the poor hermit, at each bite of the lash, would murmur, "Help me, my Lord, help me so that these blows I give unto myself begin to be a delicious contact with you . . . ! Make me suffer, Lord! Give your infinite ardor to these lashes that rend my flesh! Breathe your holy wrath into these wounds! May it sear me and make me burn like a flaming tar torch. And, suddenly, he fell down, like a dead man, with his arms flung open wide.

Full of pity, Christopher lifted him up from the ground and, as he would a dead body, moved him back inside the hut, where, still stretched out, he stayed, still emitting, from time to time, a slow moan.

The morning light grew brighter. Christopher fell asleep.

From that day forth, his service to the hermits began. Every morning, he would haul a barrel up into the rocky crags looking for a gushing stream from which he could fill it so that he could then go around, from small rustic chapel to small rustic chapel, filling their clay water jugs. Then, he would cut their firewood and knead their bread dough, which he would later bake in a brick oven next to a chapel where the saintly men would hear mass and Holy Communion. It was he who tolled the bell and who placed the woadwaxen herb on the altar — and it was also he who, on the order of the prior, scattered hard pebbles on the floor of the chapel so that the knees of the hermits would be mortified. In the afternoons, after he'd gathered together all the mats, the sandals, and the baskets that the hermits had made, Christopher would go down to the people who lived on the other side of the mountain and exchange the items made by the hands of those saintly men for flour, herbs, and wine from the cruets. All these services were easy and pleasant to do. But little by little, Christopher grew melancholy, and he began to feel a desire for the city and for the life of men. The mountain was sad and lacking in greenery, but his greatest sadness came, most especially, from its silence, and from the bitterness and the desolation of the saintly men who populated it. For them, each and every day was consumed by moaning and lamentation, even when they were working, and their constant labor was the martyrization of the body, where, for them, the Enemy had installed himself. Even when they were quiet, completely immobile, they were mortifying themselves. Some wore a belt of nails, which would tear into their flesh, while others would put ants and wasps under their tunics to bite them. Still others would suspend big rocks from their necks and would go about stumbling and gasping for air. All forms of human kindness and warmth were alien to them. In the bread that they made, they would mix dirt; their water they only wanted old and putrid. Sometimes they would stand, for days and days, without moving on top of a rock and with their arms extended and their hands spread open under the pouring rain, and when exhaustion or hunger began to conquer them, they would stick a sharp spine into their chests. Others would sleep with their heads on a stone, and with another stone on their stomachs and yet another on their legs, and they seemed like the cadavers of men so righteous that they were cut in stone. Sometimes Christopher would offer to wash their wounds, to pull the thorns from out of their feet, and to cure, by means of a mixture of water and ash, the insect bites that afflicted them. But they all rejected him, and to make their wounds more irritated, they would expose them to the burning sun or toss fine sand on them. An immense suffering covered the mountain, and over the top of it, as the wind blew its anguished moans, even the Sun seemed like a lugubrious lamp. It was, however, at night that the situation grew truly terrible. Animated by the darkness, the demons would rise up from each and every pathway to attack the saintly men. In every hovel a terrible battle would take place. The saints had their prayers and their long lashes, tipped with iron claws, but the demons, on their side, had the delicious things that all souls wanted and to which they would succumb. To the hermits who came to the battle starving, the devils would offer long tables groaning with food and covered with flowers, and where the plumes of roast peacock would flutter between heaps of fruit and blocks of ice; to those who had been great gentlemen, cavaliers, and knights, the demons showed them mountains of gold, invincible arms, great armies with which they could go forth to capture kingdoms and sack rich cities; and to the old people, they would offer miter caps, which would give them, among all men, the divine authority of holy things. And to everyone, the supreme temptation would be offered — Beauty, Woman, whether in all her magnificence, with her braids roiling down her body freely and standing erect in a gauze tunic, or delicately, hiding her naked breast with her arms and smiling fragilely.

But when these seductions did not suffice, the demons, furious, would try terror. Then, fearful serpents with vast, flabby, and putrid wings would rise up from between the rocks and, in a single blow, knock to the ground colossal figures that, streaked with white and black and brandishing three-pronged pitchforks, were spilling out a fiery drool. The cries of the hermits would resound throughout the mountain range, the horns would sound, a furious burst of prayer would be raised up to the heavens, and the leather lashes of the discipline whips would fly through the air raising many droplets of blood — and, frightened by the grandeur of the penitence, the demons would fall back, weakened, wiping away their sweat and exhausted.

A great sense of pity began to fill Christopher's heart. Why did they suffer so, those good men who plaited their baskets, who lashed themselves with their whips and switches, who went about with their faces hidden by their hoods, who did offense to no one, and who hungered only for Heaven? His only desire was to help them, to drive out, with his great strength, the black dogs of Hell that tormented them. At those moments, and at the slightest sound of a horn, he would race to the side of the besieged hermit. Panting, and with his enormous fists clenched in righteous anger, he would advance into the darkness. But where was the Devil? He would see the saintly hermit reeling in fear, he would see the dark place into which, like a lance, he would thrust the cross. . . . But if, his avenging arms poised for combat, he would then hurl himself into that place, all they would find was the darkness of the night. How many times had he found a hermit, trembling all over and murmuring to himself, "Oh, how white, and pleasing to the eyes, and full in form . . . !" Christopher understood; it must certainly be a woman, perhaps the feared Woman, who held out her curving arms and who uncovered her breasts. . . . To seize her, and to strangle her, the hermit would, gathering up his habit, virtually grovel on the ground. But his indignant hands could only grab at the gorse, and at the mosses atop a cold stone. Then Christopher himself would cry out at the terrible demons, "Come for me, come for me!" And, ripping a tree trunk out of the ground, he would throw it into the empty darkness and then flail away with tremendous blows or, tearing away a huge shard of rock, he would hurl it into the night. The tree trunks crashed against the other trees, and the rocks broke apart, with a loud cracking sound, when they struck the other rocks. And yet there was nothing in front of him except the mountain. Was it possible, then, that he'd not wounded even one of those innumerable demons who appeared there at night? Then, with the early morning light just beginning to show, Christopher, with his head bent down, would go and seek out the tracks of those fleeing devils, some piece of horn they might have left, or, on top of the singed ground, some drop of their accursed blood. But he would find only the violets, lustrous under their mantels of dew. And then he would return to the shadows of his oak trees, sluggish and yawning with exhaustion.

To celebrate their holidays, the people of the village would go up the mountain to visit the hermits. Some, ill and afflicted with all manner of ailments, and helped along by their family members, would come to implore the friends of the Lord to grant them good health. Others came to ask for his intervention in order to obtain an abundant harvest or a lost inheritance. The women would bring their children so that the brothers, by touching the heads of their children, might grant them a long, healthy, and prosperous life. And those who were sterile would come to ask that the blessing of maternity be bestowed upon them. The mountain was like a campground for pilgrims. The children, racing about, would trip on the crutches of the lame. The young girls, with flowers tucked behind their ears, formed dances in the chapel courtyards. Those who had made promises to saints dragged themselves around the cross seven times on their knees or hung wax figures, strings of ribbons, and baskets of fruit. Since they would return late to their village, almost everyone brought provisions, and, hanging their mantels on the nearby trees, they formed a big circle around the split-open watermelons and drank from wine tankards.

The hermits would come and mix with the people, though sometimes they could hardly take even their own slow, labored steps, mobbed as they were by injured or damaged supplicants who, sick of ointments and salves, asked them to touch their injuries with their crucifixes, by beggars who wanted them to cure their mange, by dropsical old women whose wombs were expecting a remedy from Heaven. Others sought only a blessing. There were also troubled faces asking for a prophecy about how the grape harvest would be. Others thrust out their rosaries so that they could be blessed. And the hermits touched the wounds, promised good harvests, and calmed the mothers of those whose souls had been possessed by the Devil.

Later, the prior climbed up to his rustic pulpit, made of rocks, and enumerated the glorious works of the mountain. Where was there, even in the Thebaid, in the sublime time of Anthony or Pachomius, a greater level of penitence? And he gestured outward to the faces emaciated by fasting and to their flesh, torn by self-flagellation. An immense admiration entranced the pious throng. And everyone wanted to see, in the bodies of those holy men, the evidence of their saintliness. And so it was then that the hermits displayed the wounds they'd made worse, the bruises that the stones on which they'd slept had given them, and the ruined teeth caused by the sour bread mixed with ashes that they ate. The women held up their arms, sobbing. The most ardent of these tore off pieces of the tunics worn by the hermits and clutched them to their breasts, like precious relics. The old people kissed the ground where the hermits had trod. In front of their huts there were crowds of people admiring the hardness of their litters, their broken pitchers, and the great notebooks. Some wanted to see the footprints of the angels that visited the hermits. Others wanted to taste their bread, or, full of respect, to touch with their fingers the discipline whips. Christopher was envied for living amongst them. Many of the people wanted to abandon their homes so they could come and serve these saintly men. And there were always some who, so that they could stay up there on the mountain, would hide themselves among the rocks, and whom it was necessary to expel when the sun began to set and it became the hour for solitude and prayer.

But on those nights, after the gatherings were finished, the prayers were not as profound, nor were the penitences as harsh. Weary, and seated at the doors to their huts, the hermits were savoring, in the silence of their hearts, their immense saintliness. Each one felt famous, spoken of in all of the homes and hearths of the valley. The fame produced by this saintliness would certainly reach the surrounding castles. The bishops would speak of them in their councils. And, later on, perhaps their images would be ostentatiously displayed above the altars. And Christopher would then see them as they gazed complacently at the wounds their penitences had caused them, as they caressed them, and as they selected a bigger, harder rock on which they could place their heads for the night. The prior then came to congratulate his brothers. His face was resplendent. And it was he who recounted the reactions of the multitude and how their wounds had been kissed. And now that he was sure of the power of his voice, he continued to speak as he climbed down to the ground and to preach against the relaxations practiced by the Benedictines. His stature grew with each passing moment. One day, as if in triumph, he even showed his brothers a letter from the Count of Occitania consulting him on the question of tithing. And Christopher became sad. He was filled with a great longing for other, more human, men, and for the laughter of children. He was especially troubled with an impatience over the vast uselessness of the hermits, their long and empty silences, the hours spent with their faces up against a stone, and with that endless contemplative immobility from which no modicum of good work would come, nothing that would warm someone's heart. Peopled by all that inertia and inaction, the mountain seemed to him to be even more lifeless and inert. And there came over him, like a wave, a desire to shake that fixedness out of those men and their things and, with his own hands, to grab them up, the hermits, the oak trees, the skulls, and the rocks all together, and push them all, headlong, down the mountain, and toward some purposeful action so that they could be useful to the world of men!

Little by little, Christopher's heart began to define itself by this form of love. No longer did he run so happily to fill their water jugs; their many crosses, clasped by so many arms, no longer led him to feel the same sweet kindness in his soul. And he hated the skulls, with their frozen rictus and offering up to the sun nothing more than their cold whiteness. And when, at night, the horns would sound, imploring the aid of the brothers' prayers, he no longer sprang to his feet, full of pity for these men. All the self-flagellation exasperated him and made him impatient. And on the feast days, he would hide himself away in the upper reaches of the mountain so he did not have to witness the vanity of the hermits as they displayed the wounds caused by their whips.

One day, the prior ordered Christopher to fashion, out of a log, a cross that was as tall as a man. He worked for three days. And when, finally, he'd succeeded in carving out the cross and placing it in a prominent spot on the mountaintop where there were no trees, the prior called to his brothers from the hermitage. One by one, they came down, praying all the while. The prior backed himself up against the cross, with his body molded to its wood, and opened his arms so that they, too, pressed up against the arms of the cross — which had now become a human cross, one glued to the wooden one. Then he ordered that a canticle be sung. When it was ended, the prior spoke: "I am going to remain here, without eating or sleeping, for three days and for the sake of the three who constitute the Holy Trinity. Glorious this work be!"

All raised their hands to Heaven, edified. Christopher, that very afternoon, descended the steep gulch to the valley below, and, without glancing back even once, abandoned the mountain forever.

xii/ Christopher took the path that was on the opposite side from where the people lived and began to walk, aimlessly, through the long ravine, which bypassed the mountain range. It was the bed of an ancient river that had once sought its bottom among the rocks but was now infinitely sad and dry. All night long he walked, in the light of a great, full moon. Come morning, he slept at the mouth of a cave he'd come upon. The solitude was that of a deserted world, one where he was the only inhabitant. Christopher dreamed of meadows and of very clear, very cold streams that ran between flowering oleanders. When he awoke, he was thirsty, and all around him there was only a ground so hard and sterile that not even gorse could grow there.

Walking ceaselessly all day long, Christopher suffered from a terrible thirst. As the sun began to set, he judged that he was seeing the sheen of what seemed to him to be a body of water. But it was only great slabs of rock, like the remains of a terrace, or the large, flat stones of some old manor house. Stretching out on the ground, he waited there for morning to come. And, after a period of uncertain sleep, he thought he'd seen the glowing eyes of wolves that were passing by and then disappearing into a nearby gully. Once daylight broke, he directed his steps toward that same gully and, moving further down it, he found some muddy and putrid water, which he drank with delight.

For two more days and nights he walked, and there was no end to the desert, with its sterile hills and dales, its steep outcroppings of rock, and its black, gravelly soil, full of cracks and fissures from being scalded under the hot August sun. Sitting down from time to time against a rock, Christopher would close his eyes out of fatigue and the intensity of the dryness, and it seemed to him that, as a fresh breeze came up, he could see great hunks of bread and pieces of fruit dropping from the trees. He would reach out to catch one but he found only hard, hot rocks. Continuing his march, and, again, without stopping, he began to suffer from hunger.

But one afternoon, as he was walking along, now so weak that his feet were stumbling at every step, he found himself at the foot of a mountain where a somber, deep-green forest grew. Christopher dove into its density. As soon as he did, he heard the murmuring of water. Pressing on, deeper into the woods, he found a thicket of oak trees laden with acorns. Christopher remained there for two days, consoling himself and slaking his thirst and hunger. Later, when he emerged from the forest, he saw before him a land full of trees, with a brook running through it, high, thick walls, and the stillness of a once lived-in place. Off in the distance, a slow trail of smoke climbed skyward into the clear air. Christopher directed his steps in that direction. The smoke was coming from a burned-out country house. Off to the side there were broken barrels, and the carcass of a half-desiccated cow that was rapidly disappearing under the buzzing of a horde of flies. The orchard had been torn up and devastated, and, all around, the soil and the plants were trampled, as if by a troop of knights on the march.

Christopher continued on, walking along the bank of the creek. Great meadows were greening up and covered in yellow-eye grass. The boughs of the willow trees dipped into the clear, flowing water. The birds were chirping in the fresh, cool air. And in the midst of this peaceful scene stood a mill, with its door smashed in and hanging from its hinges, and with the great poles of its blade wings broken and its walls scorched from the fires all about it. The mill seemed to lie there with all the sadness of a corpse in a spring meadow. Christopher headed toward the mill. Hanging from a half-split-open tree, behind the mill and next to the stairway, was an old man, with a rock tied to his feet. Off to the side were the blackened sticks of a now extinguished fire, and next to it was a forgotten lance.

Christopher continued on. All along the road were the confused steps of knights on the march. All the hedgerows were crushed and trampled down and a rustic bridge had been hacked to pieces. Other houses and huts appeared devastated, naked, with their straw roofs burnt away. And not a single living creature could be seen amongst those ruins.

At the end of a long day, however, and having sat himself down next to a ruined shack, Christopher sensed a noise among the trees. A man suddenly appeared, in rags, livid and gaunt, and then disappeared just as suddenly into the dense foliage. In order not to leave him full of fear, Christopher got up and went over to where there was a rocky hill. A great oak tree was growing at the mouth of a cave. And at the sound of his steps, the head of an old woman appeared from it . . . and then, seemingly frightened, she quickly disappeared. It pained Christopher to wonder why these people went to such lengths to hide themselves. Why would it be that this land was populated by people who hid themselves in the forest, in animal burrows, and underneath the rocky crags . . . ? Why? A great sense of pity began to come over him. When he heard the rustle of tree boughs being pushed apart, he shouted out "Peace be with you! Peace be with you!" to reassure those panic-stricken hearts. But as quickly as he did that, the parted boughs closed back up and everything was silent again.

Christopher walked on, drinking from the streams and eating acorns and the plants and herbs he found in the meadows. One day he spied a village of thatched-roof huts huddled together and spread out around a church, whose tower was under construction. He followed a path that ran between rows of sycamore trees. Moving down it, he saw a woman who, clutching a child, was searching for herbs and greens, and, upon seeing him, she fled, so frightened that she dropped the child on the ground. Christopher picked up the little one, who was so thin that its poor little bones knocked together beneath a skin that was full of sores and wounds. And yet, putting a little hand over its brow, where the wounds were biggest, it did not cry. Christopher's heart filled with pain. He yelled loudly to the woman. No one responded. Then, holding the child next to his bosom, he continued on under the sycamores. But as he did, he sensed, off in the branches along the side of the trail, that someone was following him. He sat the child on the ground and stepped off to the side. Then, turning around quickly, he saw the woman jump out from the gorse, snatch up the child, and then disappear again into the underbrush.

The village was at the end of the path. The first houses, located next to a palisade of posts, were deserted and stripped bare inside, as if they'd been sacked. There were no herds of cattle that could be seen in any of the yards. Nor were there any scythes hanging from any fireplaces.

At one door, an old woman, skinnier than a skeleton, was looking out and staring vaguely but fixedly into the distance with eyes that seemed dazed with fear. An abandoned cadaver that no one had buried had had its hands cut off. From time to time, a figure would come racing by, his hair flying. A woman, lying face down on the ground and with her hair unbound, was tied to an empty cradle. But at the far end of the village, next to a cross, Christopher could see a crowd of people milling about. An all but shoeless friar, without a hood but with burning eyes, was holding on high a cross and calling out to God for justice. How could his people suffer any more on this earth? The noblemen were making war, and this was the source of the plague that had befallen them. The barons had overrun their lands and sacked everything, robbing them of all they had in order to train and supply their soldiers and to form legions even more brilliant. If others, stronger than they, made prisoners of them, they would come round on their great warhorses to sack them yet again, to rob them, and to take from the poor their last piece of firewood and their last handful of beans so as to secure the price of their ransom. If they emerged from the strife as victors, then they would return to sack everyone else, to tear out the scarcely mature harvest so they could celebrate with days of feasting and the construction of huge mansions. Further back, and behind the main crowd, came the companies of mercenaries, who, finding nothing to their liking, set about burning the grounds, destroying the groves of trees, and killing the infants in their cradles. For how much longer would the Lord consent that such evil be visited upon the earth? Wherever Christopher went, he saw only hunger and suffering. Women were eating the bodies of their children. The men would soon become like wild beasts. And this is how it was for those who found themselves in the path of that famished mob.

Christopher's hand trembled in the air, filled, as it was, with threats and imprecations. And all about him, the young men, all livid, clenched their fists and flashed eyes that were seeking to take up arms. Others, however, merely lowered their heads. What could a poor person, all alone, do in this sterile land? Justice was supposed to come from God. But then a woman shouted, "Or maybe from the Devil . . . !" A murmuring of terror passed through the crowd.

Christopher left the village with his heart crushed. His eyes lifted themselves up unto the heavens. There, behind the blue, was the Lord! He was certainly seeing all the torments, the wars, the hunger, and the pestilence. Why did he not come down from his golden throne? A single caress of his right hand would give poor people all they needed, an abundance of fruit and bins of bread. And the black bands of cruel feudal lords would, with a wave of his left hand, disappear, like dark clouds that the sun undoes. . . . Why did the Lord not come?

The lands that Christopher was now crossing continued on, desolate, until he came to enter into a kinder and more fertile region, one with vast prairie lands and villages. He saw, off in the distance, long streams of smoke drifting upward toward the heavens. A group of soldiers were cutting down trees. And very soon after that, he saw the tents of an encampment. It was a company of vagabonds. The tents were thrown up randomly, without any kind of order, but with everyone trying to achieve the closest proximity to the river. And since it was mess time, the soldiers could be seen bending down and plunging their great iron pans into the water. Everywhere, over the blazing fires and suspended from bent steel rods, great cauldrons were bubbling. And around the carts, which were hauling the barrels of wine that had been stolen from the homes of people and from the monasteries, men were gathering with their tankards in their hands. Two butchers were skinning an ox that had been staked down to the ground. And all the work was being done in an incessant din of cursing and singing.

All of the men, filthy and with unkempt beards and big scars running across their faces, wore a short kilt made of iron mail. And since they were in a conquered land, and so felt no fear of surprise attack, their helmets and shields were hanging on poles at the front of their field tents, some of which were made of canvas while others were of sheepskin. The chief's tent, with its banners flapping in the wind, was up on a hill. Following the soldiers, women circulated throughout the encampment. Some were there because they'd been abducted in raids on their villages, while others accompanied the men for reasons of debauchery. Here and there, a monk, barefoot, possessed of a burning gaze, and with a dagger stuck inside the cord of his habit, would go from tent to tent. Some men were gambling or playing dice. Others were cleaning their weapons. Falcons screamed from atop their perches, here made of lances.

Serenely, and in the fullness of his simplicity, Christopher could cross back and forth through the camp.

And since each day the two bands of men recruited new vagrants and vagabonds, or took more serfs prisoner, no one thought his presence odd. "Who do you belong to?," they would ask. And he would make a vague gesture toward the tents. And, judging him to be an idiot, like all other giants, they would let him go on his way. Or they would take advantage of him and use his size and strength to move their hogsheads of wine, to split firewood, and to give their mules a rest by moving onto his back the heavy loads that had been tied onto their backs with ropes. Because Christopher was doing their work, he was able to eat and drink. Then night would fall and the stars would shine. Everywhere, fires would be lit. Gathering around them, the men would drink, shoot dice, or listen to a monk tell stories about the Devil. Sometimes the cry of an abused woman would cut through the air. Scurrilous songs muffled the shouts of the sentinels. And from up on the hill, where the leaders were camped, there would come the sweet music of fife play and kettledrums.

Christopher, meanwhile, moved about amongst the tents. If he saw a wounded vagabond who was trying to bandage up his wounds, he would squat down to help. For the newly captured horses that were whinnying and sticking out their muzzles in search of water, he would find a tub full. And he would unburden the women of the heavy loads of firewood that the men obliged them to haul around. But those people were evil, they burned villages, they pillaged the shrines, they beat their animals hard, and they left their children amongst the brambles on the side of the road to die from a lack of food. Christopher, very late at night, left the camp thinking, in his simplicity, that Jesus, his lord and master, did not want him to remain among those hard hearts.

For three days and three nights he walked, and, eventually, he came upon a land of great penury. The soil, dry, full of cracks, and abandoned, did not even produce thistles. Even the blooms on the trees had dried up and died. At every step, the white bones of dead animals dotted the path. The people working in the fields, whom he would come upon, had nothing more than the rags that covered their bones, and their eyes shone like those of wild animals. From time to time, along the banks of a small stream, he could see emaciated women and children crawling along and devouring tree roots. And where the land was even more nude and bereft, it was the dirt itself that they ate, by the handful and in between the tears that fell from their eyes down to their fingers. One night, as he passed by a cemetery, Christopher saw shadowy figures that, having just dug up a dead body, were carving it up into pieces next to a fire. Later on, a beggar pleaded with him for protection because those same people would attack the weakest of the poor just to have something to eat, even if that meant human flesh. Christopher bore the beggar on his shoulders for an entire day. As he did, the beggar, his teeth chattering in horror, told of parents who had eaten their small children and of others who lured travelers away from the path and killed them. At the end of that day, after he had placed the poor, lame man on the ground so that he could rest a bit, Christopher saw him sigh one final time and die. During the night, he could see, all around him, the shining eyes of the wolves, who were also starving, as they ran about gnawing on the bones of the deceased. Black bands of vultures circled overhead.

And the pain Christopher felt was so great that he stretched his arms up to Heaven and cried out to the Lord. He, certainly, was not listening. At the doors of the small country chapels thereabout, the people gathered in vain to implore mercy from on high; the saints did not come down from their altars, the relics of the martyrs seemed to have lost their strength, and so, disillusioned with Heaven, those same people were now stoning the shrines.

Who would save the people? And Christopher walked on, full of pain at not being able to save them. What good did the strength of his great arms do him, or all the goodwill in his heart?! Quickening his steps, and casting his gaze into the distance, he could do aught else except seek some way of being of service to mankind. And more than once it came to him that he should gather up all of those wretched people and feed them off his own flesh.

One day, as he was thinking this very thought, he came upon a land where he saw men digging in the hard ground while others were plowing and still others were sowing seeds. A troop of crossbowmen stood guard over the men, whom hunger had rendered scrawny. A monk, with an inkwell tucked into the waist cord of his tunic, was reading a roll of names. The abbots of the monasteries and the bishops, in council, were rounding up the strongest, healthiest men of the villages so that, for an extra ration of bread, they could be made to work the fields in order that these did not go untended and thus contribute further to the torment of hunger. These men were strong of arm but rendered dreadfully thin by famine. Their women and children had come with them so as to be able to share in their meager ration of bread. Christopher asked for a hoe and the monk, having admired the strength of his arms, directed him to a nearby field, which he was to clear of gravel and gorse. With what passion he threw himself into that labor! It was as if he'd somehow sated all of his future hungers. The torn-up gorse was heaping up in mountains alongside his huge, naked feet — and still there were moments when he would go to the aid of weakest of the men who were stumbling with the weight of the carts full of stones, or to help the most exhausted ones, from whose weary hands the hoes were starting to fall. All around them, the women, seated and motionless, with their children running about, were waiting anxiously for the men, at the end of the day, to get their ration of bread, which would be placed in a basket that was being guarded by the crossbowmen. But their hunger was so great that they threw themselves on the men while they were sowing the seeds, and, reaching into their sacks, pulled out handfuls of grain. The crossbowmen had to run over to repel the children who were shouting and racing there as well.

The eyes of Christopher were full of tears. At times, while digging in the hard earth, he would say to himself, in a low voice, "Oh, ground, give us your bread quickly! Oh, ground, have pity on us!" And at these moments the blows of his hoe would become softer, almost timid, as if he feared doing harm to the very thing he was imploring. When the bread was distributed, Christopher would take only the hard crust, dividing the rest up equally between the children and giving it to them on the sly. All of the mothers' eyes were turned on him. And the men would murmur, pensively, "You're the best. . . ." At night, Christopher would follow the workers home. Most of them were going to sleep in little sheds they had constructed along the edge of the forest. A few of them, the rare ones, were going to stretch out on bundles of straw. One tall old woman, also emaciated and very disheveled, and whose eyes glowed like live coals, was prowling about the huts, borne along by a stout broomstick. Upon confronting her black shadow as it passed in front of the moon, some of the men would gasp while others would murmur, "It's a curse!" Hurriedly, the women would put their children to bed and begin to search, amongst the piles of straw, for their brooms, for little water gourds, or for some piece of white veil. And then everyone, with some coming later than others, would disappear, in utter silence, under the trees of the forest. One night, one of these powerful creatures, with burning eyes, said to Christopher, "Come." And he, in his simplicity, took his walking stick and went. From all throughout the forest, and from underneath all its leafy boughs, one could sense the rustle and movement of a great many people walking together in utter silence. Occasionally, a prolonged cry cut through the great silence. And, faster now, dark forms were flickering along underneath the rustling foliage. It was then that Christopher came to a clearing, surrounded by old people and tall oak trees, and into which the light of the moon could scarcely penetrate. A great multitude had crowded together in it and were carrying small oil lamps and candles or some kind of smoky torch whose light danced among the branches. A vast stone table, turned white by what moonlight there was, stood in the middle of the clearing. Another shaft of moonlight then illuminated a shallow iron pan, placed next to a three-legged stool covered by the skin of a young goat. A wave of impatience seemed to agitate that black mob, where, more than once, a particular gaze glowed, like that of a wild beast in the depths of the dark forest. Then a voice, from out of the depths, would howl "Fly, fly!" And then, one after another, other voices, mournful and afflicted, would also cry out "Fly!"

At that moment, the tall, all but fleshless old crone came forward, astride her broom. Another darted out behind her, with her coarse hair flying in the wind. And another behind her, and so on until a long train of women, disheveled and with their breasts bared, and with a great, white sendal trailing along behind them in the wind, began to whirl, pitiably and with their open arms moving like tired wings, around the table. Then they began to slow until, finally, and in front of the stool, the tall old woman suddenly stopped and, raising up her arms, hurled out an invocation:

Saint Mark take ye note,
Saint Manços, be ye calm,
Grace, may there ye stick,
Hosts, may ye be pricked!

Whenever you see me
In me you'll see yourselves,
And when you don't see me
Against me you'll draw breath!

And, saturninely, the entire mob would moan out, and with the ca-
dence of a hammer falling on an anvil, the same words:

Saint Mark take ye note,
Saint Manços, be ye calm,

Suddenly, the long line of women burst into a frenzy; their hair was
tangling together, their skirts, already half torn away, became undone,
and, in a frenzy, they were shrieking, clamoring, and howling:

Whenever you see me
In me you'll see yourselves,
And when you don't see me
Against me you'll draw breath!

Faster and faster, the great pack of women whirled around, leaping to
enormous heights that sent their white underskirts up over their heads
and tangled their mops of tossing hair and that, in mid-air, knocked
together their brooms and distaffs. From the midst of the mob that
was watching this scene, great shouts and cries began to emerge. Here
and there, someone's arm would hold up a torch and shake it furiously.
Wild leaps would lead to skirts flying off in the air. There were howls of
werewolves. And running around and between the legs of an awe-struck
Christopher were large figures, like dogs, racing away with their hands
on the ground. But above all this clamor, a horn sounded. There was
then a silence so great that one could hear the leaves flutter in the slow
night wind.

Once again, the tall old woman placed herself in front of the stool,
brandishing her broom. And slowly, and in a low, guttural voice, she
began to offer this base supplication:

I invoke you and re-invoke you,
And then once more the same,
And for the sake of a sacred amulet,

Thrust into a heart,
And for the bile of the excommunicated,
And for the painted goat's head,
And for the wing of the bat,
And for the pebble in the ditch,
And for the blood of the dragon,
And for all that I bring you,
Come!

An immense cry came resounding out of the crowd: "Come!" All arms were desperately raised toward the vacant three-legged stool. And the old woman, as if possessed by a delirium, cried out, in words so sharp that they pierced the air: "Come and rise up against the Lord! Come and rise up against the Bishop! Come and rise up against the Lettered! Come and rise up against the Rich!"

And with each cry, the mob would shriek out ever more avidly, "Come! Come!" A great rustling noise came from out of the thick foliage, and suddenly there appeared on top of the table, and with his legs spread out wide, an enormous man with a long, black beard and entirely covered in black fur, which gave him the appearance of a goat. An acclamation rang out and a delirium seemed to overtake everyone. The women began to cavort about while the men shook their caps wildly, and all the while the black creature, motionless and silent, glared out at them, malevolently, with his flashing eyes. After a time, when it had once again grown quiet, the creature, extending his foot, shouted out, in a hoarse voice, "Adore me!"

Everyone then kissed his foot, which then disappeared under the long furry skins of his robe.

But then, a man, wrapped in a great, white sheet arranged like a bishop's dalmatic and wearing a black miter cap on his head, came forward, limping, to the altar to read from a book he was holding in his hands. Christopher knew him. It was the lame man who'd labored at his side, snarling out unintelligible words.

Putting the book on the altar, the man opened his arms out wide and began to celebrate a rite that, to his horror, seemed to Christopher to be like the masses held in the village where he had been born. Bent over his book, and with his hands set, the man began to mutter out a reading. Raising his arms up on high, he hailed the fur-covered black creature, and, when he was once again facing the mob, he offered them his blessing. Everyone bowed down in response. A bestial and bitter laughter crackled out from among the rabble. Stock-still, the creature, with his hands now resting on his knees, was receiving his cult. An acolyte, as young and lovely as a page, mixed a black liquid in a glass. And from the giant oaks standing all around, a black shadow fell on everyone, a shadow that, here and there, the moonlight cut into livid splotches.

As in a mass, a small bell then rang. The man wearing the miter cap received the glass vessel, made an invocation, poured a drop onto the black creature's feet, which were side by side, and drank the rest. And, dabbing at his lips with the edge of the dalmatic, he stepped up onto the stool and stood there, poised to talk, like a preacher about to deliver his sermon. There then fell on everything a great silence, one so profound that the slightest rustling of the leaves could be heard. A shaft of moonlight illuminated the bearded face of the crippled man, who at that moment began to preach.

Raising his arms on high, he asked where it was that the poor could find happiness? For them, the earth was a place of desolation. And from the time they were born to the time they were borne away to the grave, the poor could do little more than groan in slavery. From dawn to dusk they worked. And to whom did all the fruits of their labor go? To the great lords of the manors, to the bishop, and to the intendants, who always came around with their halberdiers in tow. So that the great lords could have arms, the poor went without fire and shivered during the cold nights. So that the bishop could have sumptuous banquets, the poor went without bread and grew weak with hunger. And so that the intendants could live in covered houses, the poor lived in animal burrows that they themselves had dug in the earth with their own hands. And was it from only a lack of the basic necessities that they suffered? No. They were also beaten and thrown into the depths of prisons and left to die, in torment and agony. . . . If their wives were attractive, men bearing arms would come and carry them away. If their goat gave good milk, the steward from the convent would come around and confiscate it. They had to pay to live and they had to pay to die. For the poor, there was, in the world of men, no pity. And did it exist, perchance, in Heaven? It was Heaven itself that ordered the famines and that ordered the plagues. Who would save the poor . . . ? As a powerful friend, as the one who would protect them, there was only he who dwells beneath the earth and who possesses all the powers. Only he would gather together all the children of the poor where they would be free and where neither the lance of the knight nor the bishop's crosier could touch them. Only he would teach them the cures that would free them from the plague. Only he would show them how to find treasure. Only he would make the earth come to life again. Only he would give of his own flesh so that those who were hungry would have food, so that those who were thirsty would have water. All glory to him who lives in the darkness!

And the multitude shouted back, "All glory to him who lives in the darkness!"

Then, leaping down from the three-legged stool, the lame man shouted, "It's time. . . . Come eat and drink. Love whomever you wish to love. Be free men and women in the depths of the free night . . . !"

Suddenly, two men wielding large knives appeared carrying a large roasted ram that they began to carve up. Others placed a hogshead of wine on the stone table. With a bestial clamor, the ragged mob hurled itself toward the witch-like man. The black creature bawled out, "Eat of my flesh, drink of my blood!" Bloody hunks of the animal disappeared into voracious mouths. Into earthenware mugs and into wooden cups the black wine foamed and bubbled. Some fled to another spot to devour their meat and wine in silence. Others clashed amongst themselves, like dogs fighting over a bone. The women drained their mugs of wine, which dribbled down their breasts. Other people, caught up in the joy of eating, began to dance, while also brandishing bones gnawed clean of meat. Underneath the table, skinny arms battled over the scraps.

Drunkenness warmed their souls. Rough cries burst from out of the mouths of the women. And, getting up on her feet, the great witch ordered the moon to hide itself so that the people could become even freer, there in the depths of the free night. Christopher, staying quite still and leaning against a tree, watched it all, his head hidden among the upper branches. From time to time, a shepherd, grabbing one of the women, would drag her off into the darkness. Cries of sin satisfied resounded in the black thickness of the night. The witches tore off their remaining rags and, now nude and hideous to behold, leaped astride their broomsticks and flew around and around. A tall, raven-haired woman seized Christopher and wrapped her arms around him, and, with eyes that were devouring him, said, "Come!"

Gently, he pushed the creature away. And, alone, distraught, and overwhelmed by an infinite sadness, Christopher then began to walk through the dense forest. His heart was bleeding. Those clamorous people were not friends of the Lord. Their souls were lost. But why did they suffer so? The lame man had spoken the truth. For the poor, there was only misery. The great lords and barons came with their lances, and after them the bishop with his hard crosier. And when there was nothing left for the poor, a white woman, one leaning on a white stick, would emerge. And it would be the plague. Poor mankind! Poor little children! Why did the Lord not come?

XIII /

These thoughts were in Christopher's mind as he walked on. All day he walked. He'd had neither bread nor water since the evening of the day before, and as the sun was setting he sat down on a boulder at the edge of the path and wondered where he would find his evening meal. All about him was deserted and sad. There were no roads that led to human dwelling places. Off to one side lay a great lake. The tangled, black sheaves of tall canebrakes rose up in the air. And the surface of the water, touched by the light of the setting sun, seemed golden. A flock of wild ducks was winging its way across the sky. The silence was both sad and profound.

Christopher was about to continue on his way when he heard the rumble of a group of riders coming from out of the distance. A retinue of some sort appeared on the horizon, moving slowly forward. Two crossbowmen, on foot, were marching along in front. A servant carried a bundle of torches to be used when night fell. And coming right after them was a great litter, with curtains of red leather and plumed mastheads at the corners.

Two ladies, alongside the litter, were mounted on white mules. Surrounding them were armed knights with their lances at the ready. And two other mules, also plumed with red banners, bore the baggage boxes.

Christopher, now standing up, humbly took off his cap. Upon seeing his enormous, disheveled form, in the clear, golden air of the afternoon, one of the ladies cried out and the two halberdiers, coming to a halt, readied their crossbows. The litter had come to a stop and, from between the curtains, a very elderly lady, enveloped in furs, peered out, putting her hand, covered in a hunting glove, in front of her eyes. But Christopher, again humbly, had already taken a knee. The lady then gave an order — and, rudely, a squire ordered the enormous man to come closer. He then approached them, moving in between the knights, whose tall lances, standing upright from their saddles, did not come up to his broad shoulders. And from between the still unclosed curtains of the litter the elderly lady, another lady, younger and paler, and a child, as blond as an angel, looked out fearfully. And when they asked him to what seigneurial manor he belonged and why he was walking along alone on the road, Christopher, in his simplicity, could only mumble that he came from far away and that he was hungry. The younger lady touched her leather money pouch, and the child shouted, "He's the giant who served Roland!" All around them, the knights laughed, albeit with great respect. And then, suddenly, the little lord, seated on the elderly lady's knees, asked, with the charm of a mime, if he, too, could have a giant, one who would follow him with a cudgel wherever he went. The elderly lady smiled. And, without hesitation, she ordered the knights to bring Christopher along with them. With a gesture, he was commanded to march alongside the baggage. And once again the little bells on the mules began to jingle as the retinue slowly proceeded on. The sun set. The squires lit the torches. And at every instant, from between the curtains of the litter, there appeared the blond head of the child, who peered out wanting to see if his giant was indeed coming along. Christopher had discovered, from the stablemen, that these people were the lords and ladies of the castle, Riba Dona, that was located beyond the lake.

Before long, high towers could be seen, up on a ridge and rising up from out of a dense forest that ran down into the valley below. At the top of the tallest tower was a flame that flickered in the wind. Long trumpet calls could be heard. And at the entrance to the drawbridge, innumerable torches appeared, borne aloft by more squires.

The intendant, the steward, two friars with habits, along with other knights and gentlemen, awaited them at the inner courtyard. Clear, bright light shone brilliantly from out of the ogival windows. And the chapel bell pealed happily. A squire, whose white beard tumbled down over a white, leather bodice, received into his arms the blond child, whom the ladies-in-waiting greeted with great courtesy, bowing down deeply in their long-tailed and fur-edged gowns. A rug had been rolled out over the vast stairway. The palace dogs were barking happily. And beneath the great door, over which hung a coat of arms, a chambermaid waited with a silver pitcher in her hands, while others, off to the side, held shining basins and fine, white towels. The enormous train of the gown worn by the elderly lady who had been holding the child's hand disappeared through the huge door. The stablemen led the horses away by the reins as others collected the lances. And the knights, whose spurs clicked and clattered over the courtyard stones, were telling the intendant and the priest how the journey had been a good one and how, thanks to the Lord, it had been without incident, with neither bulls nor werewolves.

In the meantime, all the servants had, fearfully, encircled Christopher. Humbly, he twisted his hat in his hands. The pages laughed at his unruly mop of hair and at the immensity of his dirt-covered feet. Even the kitchen help had come running to see him. The frightened dogs barked.

But one page came running up to Christopher to tell him that he was to go to the castle armory. And passing through an arched hallway, which he could traverse only by bending over at the waist, and through oaken doorways that scarcely allowed him to pass, the page took him to a room as large as a church nave. Bundles of lances were stacked against the walls. Banners were hanging from the ceiling beams, and in the back there was a huge fireplace, ablaze with big chunks of wood cut from tree trunks, and around which the knights, standing up, could warm their hands. A curtain was raised and the two ladies appeared with the child between them, and followed by more pages who were bearing wax torches.

The little lord of the castle (which he was because his father had died, two years earlier, in the war against the king of Occitania) would, by Christmas, be six years old, and, to Christopher, he seemed as delicate and as blond as the Christ Child on the chapel altar had been. But, ever since he was a baby, he had been educated to one day become a powerful knight. Every morning, his lips were pressed against a piece of blessed gold so that his words would always be honest and shining; his clothing, dried by the fire, was hung over the sharp edge of a huge sword so that he would grow up to be strong and comfortable with weaponry; and, every morning, he would bring to his neck a piece of the Holy Cross so that his heart would always be filled with Heaven's love. His favorite thing had always been to hear the stories of the paladins. At night, he would dream of Roland and stretch out his arm to take hold of the great trumpet that his hero had blown in Roncesvalles. And he yearned to free damsels imprisoned in castle towers, to conquer dragons, and to be served by a giant armed with a club.

And now he had him, his own giant, one greater than all those of whom he had heard people speak, in the winter evening get-togethers, and from the troubadours who would pass through seeking alms, or the pilgrims who had seen the marvels of the Holy Land. Directly, and with his little hand placed securely on his belt and his gaze shining ever more brightly, the young king stood in front of Christopher — who was smiling broadly, with his large, bearded face bowed down and full of tenderness for the boy. Then, pointing his finger upward and toward Christopher's shoulder, the blond lad said, very seriously, "I want to climb up there."

His tutor, taking him into his arms, then held him up, but it was not high enough. The ladies laughed; as did the knights, running their fingers through their beards. Christopher then delicately took hold of the child and, lifting him up, placed him on his huge shoulder. From that vantage point, up on high, the child beamed as he gazed down upon everyone beneath him, so small now as they stood next to the giant's knees. He spurred Christopher's shoulder and shouted, "Walk!" And Christopher marched across the room. To get past them, the boy dodged the banners hanging from the beams. His eyes, full of pride, shone like stars. But his anxious mother, down below, was wringing her hands, and calling out, "Ruperto! Ruperto!" And the tutor, standing up on the tips of his toes, stuck out his arms to take Ruperto, who had started to climb down, laughing and without fear.

The elderly lady then gave an order to the steward, and Christopher was taken to the kitchen. There, the pages and the servants ran to see Christopher, seated now on the ground, with a clay bowl full of wine on his knees and crumbling up a big piece of cornbread that a little servant boy, on a leash, had brought him.

Stretched out, that evening, in an old, abandoned stable, Christopher felt a great peace come over him. A kind of warmth had enveloped him, one that came less from the fresh straw in which he was lying than from the vague feeling that someone esteemed him, that someone liked and wanted him, and that someone needed him. It was that child, so lovely and so noble, and with his long, golden hair. And all night long, he dreamed that a boy just like that, one whose blond locks fell down over his white shirt and covered him in a golden aura, would climb all over him, starting at his toes and moving up the length of his body, as if on an uneven road that makes its way over mountains and valleys. His little feet would scarcely cease their movement. And once the child would get to his face, he would stop and, bending over to peer into Christopher's eyes, he would seem to contemplate two lakes, as tranquil and clear as a mirror. Later, in the same stillness and now climbing down his body, the boy would withdraw to the tips of his feet, from which he would be elevated into the air so he could slide down an oblique moonbeam that was shining in through a crack in the ceiling.

At the first light of dawn, before the trumpet call from the sentries that announced the new day, Christopher, leaving through an open door, went out to look over the castle and its grounds. Never had he seen such magnificent structures. A long wall surrounded the entire hilltop. Water lilies flourished in the moats. And lying beyond were vast forests and cultivated fields, through which a river, covered at that hour in mist, snaked its way between great groves of poplar trees.

Peace had reigned in those manorial lands for so long a time that green plants were growing in the fissures of the drawbridge. Thanks to the mercy shown by the great ladies who governed there, the beams of the gallows were rotting from disuse and covered in green moss. And out from above the main turret was a lance skewering a visor-less helmet and a water dipper, signifying that there both pilgrims and knights would find not strife but hospitality. Towers rising up from sharply angled roofs were innumerable, and all had red and green banners or pennants that waved in the breeze. On top of the battlements, dragon-shaped figures, bending over, would vomit out the rainwater. And in every ogival window, with each one bearing an escutcheon, there was a scarlet vase in which a lily was growing.

Inside the walls, everything was magnificent. The courtyard stones, polished like those of a church, were surrounded by an earthen enclosure where rosebushes grew. The well was topped off by a dovecote, which culminated in an image of Saint Mark where the doves came to rest, billing and cooing on top of his great, open book. Behind one tower, black and isolated from the others and which served as the castle treasure house and archive, there was a garden in full bloom. And off to the side, there was a covered garden where games of ball could be played and a low lane for jousting competitions. And in the tranquillity of that ladies' manor house, so alien to the things of war and respected throughout the extensive environs, the sentinels, up on the parapets, played at dice or slept like sated friars.

Christopher was gazing about in astonishment at these marvels when a page approached and summoned him to an audience with the intendant. In a great arched room, and seated on a giant chair of carved oak that stood in front of a table covered in rolls of parchments and notebooks stamped with coats of arms, the intendant explained to Christopher the nature of his obligations and duties, which would be to accompany the young master, on foot and alongside his horse, everywhere he went and armed with his club. Soon after this, a hunchbacked man entered the room and, climbing deftly up onto a chair, measured Christopher with a wooden ell, from the top of his head to the bottom of his feet. Then, he departed, bowing over and over, with his pack of scissors, shears, and pincushions tinkling at his waist.

With the taking of his measurements completed, Christopher later received orders to carve a great cudgel from out of a tree trunk and to accompany the young ruler of the castle on a visit he wanted to make to his forest lands. Resplendent, now, in his new clothes, as he awaited his lord and master on a clear August morning, Christopher could not cease from looking at himself in the clear water of the cistern. He was stupefied at seeing his legs now covered in breeches made of blue-and-red-striped cloth and with a red-and-blue doublet covering his chest and embroidered with his lordship's coat of arms.

In a short time, the youthful monarch then appeared, mounted on a white colt and with white plumes adorning his hat, out from underneath of which his blond locks came tumbling down. Walking alongside him, a tutor carried a falcon on his fist. And two knights, with their lances at the ready, followed behind them. Upon seeing Christopher, the child cried out in joy. And three times he made the colt, which was afraid, circle about Christopher, who stood very still, resting his club on his shoulder. A short time later, having crossed over the drawbridge, the young master headed down the long road that stretched out before them, turning around lightly and sprightly in his saddle now and then to watch Christopher, who was trotting along behind him with his giant steps and his long, tangled mop of hair blowing about in the wind. From out of the doors of the huts and hovels along the road, the manor's peasants knelt down in homage to their lord and master, who tossed them handfuls of copper coins from his money pouch. And immediately after that, these same peasants, now en masse and with their arms stretched out, would gaze in wonder at the giant who was running along behind.

At the end of the ride, when he'd stopped and dismounted in a clearing where a tower rose up, the boy refused to get back on the colt and, instead, insisted that he return to the castle riding Christopher. In vain, and pleading on one knee and holding the colt by the reins, the tutor begged the young lord to get back on his horse. With a determined look, the boy would only say, "But I want to!" And, sighing, the elderly tutor helped him climb up to Christopher's neck, which he then mounted, fixing his spurs in their leather covering. At that moment, the boy's happiness was extreme. It was as if he had climbed up to the very top of a great tower. Spurring him forward, he then made Christopher stop so he could pick the topmost strawberry tree flowers, which he then tossed down to the people below; then he wanted to look into the bird nests; and finally, prodding Christopher's chest and making him run, he clutched the giant's hair as if he were holding the reins of a great warhorse. And in this fashion he returned to the castle, where, on the magnificent stone veranda his mother and grandmother, awaiting him, were wringing their hands and wavering between a state of anxiety and one of delight at seeing the boy ride the giant like that, just as in the tales the minstrels told.

And from that day forth, the boy's greatest happiness was to ride Christopher. There were then great outings, around the walls of the castle grounds or the moats, but sometimes much longer, as far as the outlying forests. Christopher always trotting, the boy always laughing. And thus, little by little, did the boy come to grow fond of Christopher, just as he would a horse that understood him and that made him laugh, with violent bucking and a long, undulating gait, like that of a giant dromedary. Christopher, too, little by little came to give his entire heart to the child. When he felt him up on his shoulders, his entire face would light up. No matter how hard the boy would pull his hair, Christopher felt only the caress of his hands. To make him laugh, Christopher would whinny and neigh like a real charger. Or, pretending to be frightened, he would not want to go forward, and the boy's spurs would rake his leather tabard. On rainy days, when the boy didn't leave the castle, Christopher would spend the entire time milling sadly about the courtyards, lost in the melancholy of his idleness. And at night, he would not return to his stable, where otherwise his eyes would be cast on the window through which he could see the light that illuminated the boy.

Other times, however, the boy wanted Christopher to come dine with him. And on those occasions, two pages would open up the great tapestries even wider so that Christopher could enter into the great hall, with its ceiling painted blue and sprinkled with flowers that shone brilliantly, as if set out in gold. Standing motionless, over in a corner, Christopher contemplated the boy, who was seated next to his grandmother in a chair as high backed and ornate as hers. Behind them, the tutor was taking the plates and dishes from the hands of the squire. On top of the table, covered in fine linen, the silver tumblers jingled and tinkled. The buffets groaned and bowed under the weight of the food and tableware. A great blaze was dancing in the fireplace, over which the amphitheater of Antioch was depicted. And atop their perches, made of polished iron, the falcons sharpened their beaks.

Sometimes, though, the boy wanted Christopher closer. On those occasions, his mother would make a dry gesture of resignation — and Christopher, in great humility and cowed by the manorial splendor, would draw nearer, bowing down and with his cap in his hands. The boy would want him down on his knees, with his hands on the ground, and he would tap him on the back and hold out morsels of meat to him, which he would then eat noisily, this adding greatly to the boy's amusement.

Other times, at night, a page would come to get Christopher and take him to the kitchen, and they would enter into a large room with a roaring fireplace, where they would sit down. Seated in her chair, the grandmother would have the Book of Hours open on her lap and with the boy at her side. In front of them, his mother would be working on a tapestry. And a troubadour, at her feet and seated on a footstool, would be recounting a long romance of chivalry and love. There was always a paladin bearing great, black arms, a damsel imprisoned in some tall tower, and a giant guarding the door to an enchanted castle. And the boy would exclaim, "I, too, have a giant!"

And he would order Christopher, who seemed monstrous, with his huge knees clearly illuminated from the flames of the burning logs and his head nearly hidden in the shadows of the ceiling beams, to stand up. The friar would raise his sleepy eyelids and the lady would pause with her long needle suspended above her tapestry. And all, looking at Christopher, felt more real and as though they themselves were living the long story of fairies, enchanters, and knights in armor that they were listening to. And later on in the evening, the squires would serve dry cakes and tankards of mulled wine.

Thus did tranquil days pass in the tranquil castle. Without variation, the lookout, upon announcing the break of day with a salute from his horn, would then run up the main tower mast the great silk banner that carried the lord's coat of arms. The castle windows would open up, the sacristan would sweep out the chapel, the barnyard servant would appear carrying his milk cans, and the pages, singing away like newly awakened birds, would come running down the steps to play at ball games or they would head to the covered tilting field where the master-of-arms was testing the swords and evaluating the bend of their blades or checking the iron of the lances.

If the weather was clear, the ladies and the boy would take walks through the upper terrace lands. The child, leaning over, would sometimes shout for Christopher to come while the ladies would breathe in the fresh, cool air or watch the flights of the new falcons that the falconers were training.

At midday, two trumpeters would announce lunch for the ladies and gentlemen, while at the great door of the castle the manor's poor would gather, with their hands out, to get, after the others were finished, the leftover bread or the bones of the fowl consumed.

Every so often, in the afternoon, the jangling of little tambourines and bells would announce the arrival of a company of minstrels and jesters. One of them, with his cap in his hand, would ask for permission to put on a show in the courtyard. The ladies would gather on the balconies, the pages would all come running, the archivist would stick his head out of one of the tower's windows, and the cooks would peer out from between the latticework of their windows. And out in the courtyard, the jesters, juggling balls, dancing to the accompaniment of stringed instruments, lifting weights, or playing out farces, elicited great "oohs and aahs" of marvel and delight from the crowd. When they were finished and about to depart, one of them would always call out to Christopher and discreetly gesture to him — and once safely outside the drawbridge try to persuade him to go off with them, to enjoy their carefree and happy life and to travel among the castles, visit the fairs, go into the cities, and to gather up money for old age. With a slow shake of his head, Christopher would always refuse. And they would head off down the road, all the while looking back at him and calculating all the profit they would gain from putting that giant on exhibit.

Other times, it was a posse of nobles that came into sight. The courtyard would resound with the snorting and neighing of their great mounts. The pages, bustling about, would come running. Rugs were thrust out of the windows and beaten clean, and in the kitchens, the main chef, hot and red faced like a pimento, would be preparing great meat and vegetable turnovers, out of which live doves would come flying. On those days, the boy would be filled with pride as he showed off Christopher, his giant. And, in front of the astonished nobles, Christopher would gallop around, like a horse, with the boy on his shoulders. And the guests' chaplain would take Christopher's measurements so his story could be later told to others.

Still other times, and occasionally in the dark of night, there would sound at the castle doors a trumpet of war. And a knight would enter, silent, covered in iron armor, and accompanied by a squire. A chambermaid would come running to offer him a jug of perfumed water to wash his hands. A page would relieve him of his lance while another marched ahead carrying a wax torch to lead the way in. And the knight, carrying his helmet in his hands and shaking his hair, would, as befits a paladin, sonorously call out his name as one renowned in those lands. Or it would be a pilgrim who'd come to the door, one whom the squires would immediately lead to the kitchen where he could lay down his mantel next to the fire so that any dampness it had acquired from the road might be dried away. Christopher would always, and with great respect, secure his walking stick, from which a gourd drinking cup might hang. Very soon, a chaplain would appear and conduct him to an audience with the ladies, to whom he would tell of his travels and of the marvels of the Holy Sepulcher — and Christopher waited, hoping to be able to kiss the hem of his garments, which had touched the tomb of the Lord.

And so the years passed. The child was becoming a young man, and he began to receive instruction in the arts of the hunt and of war. Every day, the huntsman would bring him extra hounds, to fill out his pack of hunting dogs, and mules would arrive bearing boxes that contained ornate, inlaid arms which the boy was to learn to wield. But, because of the wishes of the grandmother, who was given to the joy of learning, the boy would spend long hours with the chaplain, who would instruct him in letters, in mathematics, and in writing his name on parchments. Little by little, the boy lost his curiosity about Christopher. Sometimes, he would even pass by him without smiling or without waving to him with his hand, which was now always covered with a small hunting glove.

But Christopher did not live in idleness. The pages would give him arms to clean and polish, and the sacristan, now old and hobbled, would ask him to sweep out the chapel — and it was also he who lit the ovens in the kitchen and who washed the dirty tableware. One day later on, the grandmother, reading a story in which a giant stood guard over a great treasure, asked Christopher to guard the tower, where the archives and money coffers were kept. From then on, the tower was in his care. He kept a constant vigil over it, even cleaning it and clearing it of moss and weeds. Every morning and afternoon, he would tap on the latticework of the tall, narrow windows to make sure no iron work had come loose or unfastened. And it was he who carried both lunch and supper up to the archivist, who was always bent over his parchments. And now Christopher would sleep at the tower door with the great, iron key clutched in his hand. Even so, the boy did still sometimes want to be trailed by Christopher. These were his happiest days. Like a half-abandoned dog, his simple, good eyes implored the boy for a bit of kindness. But, before long, the boy would, with a gesture, dismiss him, for now he was only interested in arms, falconry, and warhorses. And Christopher, sighing and with a heavy heart, would stretch out on the ground next to the tower with the thick, heavy key resting on his knees.

One day, not long after that, a family relative arrived at the castle and bearing a present for the child, a disfigured dwarf. He was only slightly taller than an arrow shaft and had an enormous head and evil eyes. His long, thin, and raspy beard gave the appearance of being like the chin whiskers of a goat. The boy became entranced by his dwarf and never again gazed upon Christopher.

Christopher's pain was immense. For him, the castle had suddenly become as cold and deserted as a hilltop buffeted by the cold north winds. All day long his eyes scoured the places the boy would go, the doors through which he would pass, even the arena where he would hone his archery skills. And when the lad would appear, Christopher would hide himself among the towers, not wishing to show that he knew he was not wanted or out of fear that he would not be called to, with a happy laugh, as in earlier times. And, in his simplicity, he would think to himself, "What have I done? Why does he no longer like me?" Every night he dreamed of the boy. It was always the same child, with his blond locks falling down over a very white shirt, who would climb all over his body, but, instead of coming to gaze upon his face, he would only come to bury the point of his arrow in the place he felt Christopher's heart beating, and he would do so in a particularly dry and cruel manner.

Seated at the door of the tower, and contemplating that ingratitude, Christopher sighed deeply several times. And, upon hearing those sad sounds, the archivist inclined his bald head through the window shutter and looked down. To try and be at least a little bit involved with the boy's life, Christopher was the one who cleaned and tended to his favorite colt, sometimes even kissing its muzzle. For Christopher, the saddle in which the boy rode, the velvet-covered reins, and his silver stirrups were sacred objects, which he would touch with the greatest devotion.

One morning, at about this time, a sense of great concern swept over the castle. The boy had fallen ill. Two pages galloped off almost immediately, and it was not long before the physician, mounted on his mule and carrying his box of drugs, arrived. What followed were days of uncertainty and unease. Day and night, the chapel was alight with burning candles and full of governesses praying. From a nearby convent came relics of Saint Teódulo. The pages, who now neither played at ball nor quarreled, only whispered, fearfully, off in the corners. Others set out to traverse the pilgrim trails and those of the peddlers in quest of some new or hitherto unknown cure that these people might have encountered on their distant travels. Christopher didn't sleep. All night long, his eyes were focused only on the windows of the boy's bedroom. Trembling, he would ask the chambermaids about the boy's condition. He would go out among the servants and the peasants living in the thatched huts and inquire about medicinal herbs. Later, he even went to consult a herdsman who was allegedly also a shaman. And so that no noise could disturb the boy, Christopher would go out at night, armed with his staff, and beat the water in the moats so that the frogs would stay quiet.

One day, however, the boy appeared on the castle terrace, supported on either side by the two ladies. He was still pale, but he was smiling at the bright winter sun. Waving their caps in jubilation, the servants and servers all ran to greet him, though respectfully remaining some distance away. The chapel bell pealed happily. And Christopher, with his hands pressing together in supplication, waited anxiously in the hope that the boy's eyes would fall upon him. The boy approached the terrace balcony — and his eyes, still vague and sad, surveyed the crowd but without even once coming to rest on the giant. Christopher returned to his tower, with two big, heavy tears running down his face and into his beard.

At that moment, the castle, for him, had lost all of its enchantment. And so it was that, as if he had ended up suffocated by living in amongst those high towers, his thoughts now returned to the open fields and the dwelling places of the humble people among whom he'd been born. Since the peace that had long reigned there was so great and profound, none of the castle's guard duties was now being performed with precision and exactitude. Like friars dozing off in the convent waiting room, the sentinels would fall asleep up on the turrets, the doormen would leave their bundles of keys dangling out in the open on the iron door knockers, and the tower with the archives was thought not even to need guarding. As soon as he would get it swept out, Christopher, taking his staff in hand, would head off through his master's feudal lands and walk among the hovels of the tenant farmers and serfs.

They all knew him. Among them, there was always a tankard of wine for him, and Christopher would play with the children or help with shearing the lambs. Little by little, he became everyone's helper, and, as in earlier times in his village, it was he who carried the heavy packs, who split the wood, who repaired the roofs, and who tilled the hardest ground. Sometimes, he would even tend the flocks or look after the mills. At night, he would rest among those poor people but with no regret over the good things he had enjoyed in the castle, like the fresh bread and the generous portions of salted meat. Gathered together with one of the families at their hearth, Christopher would often spend an already darkening late afternoon watching the fire as the children roasted chestnuts and potatoes in the hot ashes. And, as he was in the midst of those humble people, Christopher would listen to them as they talked, slowly and gravely. The oldest would tell stories about the old count, a cruel man who, out in the fields, would spur his horse against the laborers or lay waste to the orchards and gardens. People said that he had a pact with the Devil, and many said they'd seen him hunting at night, in torchlight and guided by a figure all dressed in red who would blow a trumpet out of which flew sparks and fire. During other, more peaceful times they told of seeing him with the other count, the one who had died in the war, and out with the ladies — how merciful they were! — and whose gallows were rotting away. But then they would tell of how greatly oppressed they, the poor, were by that tall castle, with its coats of arms and pennants! And of how hard their lives were and how they were still subjected to endless and brutal labor. And each one would recount his miseries, the incessant slaving away, the scarce bread, the children broken in health by the cold and by want, the hunger they suffered and that came at them as if with the teeth of wolves. . . . Their voices would become sadder and sadder. The cold wind would blow in from the cracks in the walls of their homes. And the mothers, sighing, would rock the cradles, where slept their innocent children, destined to suffer the same servitude and the same misery. Christopher, with his infinite compassion, felt his heart well up in pain.

From time to time, a mendicant monk would come knocking at the door. One such man, upon entering their dwelling, gave everyone his blessing and then, dropping his rucksack in a corner, went over to the hearth to warm his feet, which, lacerated by the sharp thorns of the heather, were sore from his journey. In the heat of the fire, his coarse brown cotton-cloth habit, damp from the road, gave off steam. The son of peasants, and born out in the fields, he knew the misery of the poor people. And, poor monk that he was, he, too, suffered from oppression, and from the vanity of the wealthy prelates, with their castles, their chaplets, and their well-armed soldiers. Then, seated on the best stool, and with his rosary dangling down between his knees, he, too, spoke of the misery of their time and place. Our Lord, certainly weary of such iniquity and wickedness on the part of his great and powerful people, would not delay in returning to earth to better distribute his bread, to reform his orders, and to lessen the pride and vanity of rich men! And who knows? Incomprehensible are the ways of Providence! Perhaps, to punish the castles, God might raise up in revolt an army from out of the hovels. A simple cattle prod will penetrate the best armor — when it's the hand of Saint Michael the Archangel who thrusts it. Perhaps here on Earth there could be repeated, in miniature form, the cosmic battle between the Archangel and the Devil. There was talk, he said, that a great fire had already raced across the sky, passing from west to east. And out at sea, a scythe and a lance, upright and crashing together, was said to have been seen. And then, lowering his voice, he told how, in the royal lands he'd passed through, men were gathering together, under cover of night, and laying plans to put an end to forced servitude.

Pensive, Christopher returned to the castle. To him, all those towers and walls seemed to have a cruel aspect to them, and to be hostile to the poor. Why could there not be the same hearth for everyone, the same bread? Those great treasures in the tower, the ones he guarded, could become a horn of plenty for the little children of the earth. And why were there so many arms? What were they for? Men should not fight each other; they should only embrace each other, in peace and harmony.

One day, as he was having such thoughts, and as he was seated next to the moat, an old man came passing by, prodding his burro, heavily laden with herbs and greens. He was one of the castle serfs. He seemed to be in a hurry, and in his face a degree of uneasiness could be seen. On seeing Christopher, he stopped, saying "New evils, new evils!" And since Christopher was staring wide-eyed at him, the serf continued to speak, telling of how, down in the market, where he'd come from, there was talk that a band of poor people had arisen in a neighboring territory, one further off, on the other side of the hills, and that it had as its rallying cry, "Death to the castles!" Other people, other serfs and workers, were said to be picking up their cattle prods and joining forces with them.

The entire land seemed to be in revolt. Two castles had already been attacked, the ladies and the children killed, and now two towers up on their hill were burning. And, without saying another word, he prodded his herb-laden burro and fled. Immediately, Christopher stood up and followed him. When, trailing after the old man, he arrived back at their village, there were already groups of people gathering in the churchyard and talking, in hushed voices, in the doorways of their homes. The news had reached them on the wind, and everyone was afraid. On the faces of the young men there were expressions of concern and uncertainty about whether they, too, should take up their scythes and their hoes and turn their field implements into arms and join up with their brothers in servitude to avenge the plight of the poor. The older men, showing great prudence, shook their heads, no. What good would it serve to do so? The barons, crashing down upon them astride their great coursers, would always win. And the women, uneasy and anxious, remembered the goodness of the ladies of the castle, their many alms, and the pieces of lamb that, at Christmastime, they would give out to everyone. What would happen to them if the castle were attacked? There would be no soldiers to defend them, nor arms for them to defend themselves. Poor ladies, so alone and so helpless! Poor little lord, so weak and so alone!

Christopher listened in silence. And, still in silence, he then returned to the castle. For that entire afternoon, he milled about its walls, as if studying their strength and their capacity to withstand an attack. Then, with his powerful fists, he pounded on the castle doors. And since, just at that moment, the intendant was passing by, followed by his great guard dog, he asked, "What are you doing, Christopher?"

The other responded, "Bad people from the countryside are coming. You've got to raise the bridge."

The intendant smiled and shrugged his shoulders. And that night he made the ladies laugh, telling them about the giant's fears. Christopher, however, could not sleep. High up, in the tower keep, he remained vigilant all night long, watching over the surrounding countryside. In the distance, and up on a hilltop, he could make out something like camp fires. But no sounds could be heard, except for those of the toads down on the ground. When dawn broke, Christopher came down. And going to where the innkeepers were, he picked up two enormous iron bars, which, now unused, had once served to reinforce the doors. Later, the chapel bell rang, calling people to mass in the fine morning air. The archivist came and sat down among his notebooks and the ladies distributed the day's work to the servants and to the women who spun the cotton and wool into fabric. And the entire castle was reposing in the saintly peace of a Sunday. Suddenly, a page, who, up on the battlements, had been making a bird snare, let out a shout that woke up the halberdiers who'd been asleep at their stone sentry posts. Then, a trumpet sounding the alarm rang out. The pages all raced to the battlements. The ladies disappeared behind the windows of the upper balcony. And the cooks poured out into the courtyards, with their pots and pans in their hands.

Very soon came the cry that a band of armed men was advancing on the castle. The pages ran, in confusion, to the armory to grab up swords and lances. The guards in desperation locked the doors. And the intendant, his hair flying in the wind, shouted out that pitch and coal tar were to be heated up so that they could be poured down upon the mob if it tried to scale the walls. But, in the general chaos, no one was listening. The long period of peace had rendered the inhabitants of the castle unaccustomed to maintaining discipline and readiness. There was not a single knight who could take command. And the women, who had softened their hearts, ran, sobbing, to the chapel.

Suddenly, a great clamor resounded up on the walls. Christopher climbed up to the battlements — and saw an immense band of men, serfs in rags, furiously charging the castle and brandishing scythes, goads, and torches and beginning to pour over the drawbridge, which no one had remembered to raise. Others, all around them, were with great ax blows destroying the moss-covered gallows and attacking the stone bar of justice that stood underneath the seigneurial elm trees. Already, ax blows were thudding against the castle door and causing great chunks of wood to fly into the air. An enormous tree trunk, borne along by innumerable hands, was readied and brought forward as a battering ram to be sent, like a great horned sheep, crashing against the main door. From up above, the halberdiers, with hands that were none too steady, were loosing their arrows on the men below. With every cry of a newly wounded man, the mob grew more enraged and the ax blows redoubled ... until finally the old door, now splintered, began to fall open. At that moment, the halberdiers and pages descended from the battlements to take refuge in the tower. And Christopher, clutching the iron bars in his hands, also now ran to the manorial tower. Inside, in the great domed hall, the ladies were pale and seated next to each other, with the little monarch, all but hidden from view because of their garments, between them. The old steward was on his knees, praying. And all around them lay huge piles of open notebooks, the archives of the house and its line, the great genealogical tree, everything that formed the honor and pride of that family. It was as if the very citadel of feudalism was coming to its end, as if everything that defined that kind of life was finished, the hopes of a great house, its titles, its treasures, and all its pride. And all that was being threatened by a plebeian revolt!

Christopher had gone, humbly, to take up a position in the back of the domed hall. And so great was their terror, and so deep their scorn for the serfs and servants, that the lords worried neither about him, Christopher, nor about the powerful aid that his indomitable strength could be, but only about the swords in the hands of the pages, at whom they were screaming to defend the door for them.

Across the courtyards, in the meantime, the cries of the wounded could be heard over the tumult of the Jacquerie mob, which surged forward like a great wave bursting through the dikes that sought to hold it back. [The term Jacquerie references the peasant revolt in fourteenth-century France; see foreword by Carlos Reis.] And scarcely had the door of the tower been slammed shut when powerful ax blows fell upon it, and in the midst of howls of rage and terror, the sound of windows breaking and the cries of the murdered serfs could be heard. Inside the tower, no one spoke. All eyes were fastened on the door that was being attacked. Its ancient oak wood, the carvings in it, and the rusty iron plates that held it in place were their only defense against certain death. The pages, paler than wax, softened by years of peace, and lacking a warrior's education, had formed in front of the ladies a wall of swords — swords whose tips were trembling. The chaplain was bent over, praying. And the archivist had stretched his arms out over the top of his notebooks, as if to protect them. His eyes, too, were fixed on the door, and he shuddered at every ax blow. Only the grandmother seemed serene, sustained by her pride and the strength of her heart and prepared to meet her death. At the same time, her daughter-in-law, clutching the child, had succumbed to fear and was bathing him in tears. And on the winding stairway that climbed upward to the main floor, the servants and the nursemaids were huddled, some still clutching in their hands the toy rattles of the children under their care.

Finally, and under the weight of the desperate blows assaulting it, the door was giving way! Smoke from the fires lit by the Jacques outside started to pour in through the fissures in the walls. Stoked by the furniture the mob had dragged from the castle, the emblazoned chairs and even the linen chests, these conflagrations were then used to further attack the castle. No one inside counted on living for much longer. Two elderly nursemaids, rosaries in hand, begged for absolution from the priest, who, paying them no attention, was down on his knees and trembling in fear as, chanting his misereres, he pleaded for mercy.

Suddenly, the door gave way completely, crashing down on its burst hinges. And, in a frenzy of murderous rage, a welter of cattle goads, scythes, livid faces, and emaciated arms burst through into the great hall. The ladies had fled. And then, just as a powerful old man, wielding a scythe in each hand, leaped forward, over the fallen door, Christopher, seeming now to be enormous and with his face on fire, and gripping an iron bar in each hand, surged forward from out of the depths of the room.

He was like an apparition — and the furious mob drew back in terror. It was as if there had surged up against them, visible and tangible in form, that monstrous giant, the keeper of the tower, that they, now pale from fright, had heard about in the stories told around the firesides. And seizing on the moment of fear that he saw in their eyes, Christopher threw himself against the rioters, who recoiled in confusion, pulling back with their prods and scythes. Lowering his head, Christopher, towering above the others, burst out the doorway and, now standing in the great, open air of the courtyard, his dark figure, covered in a wolf's hide and with two burning eyes glaring out from underneath the bushy walls of his eyebrows, he seemed to have come from Hell itself and to be possessed of an invincible strength. His roars made the walls quake — and his two iron bars, hissing furiously, slashed back and forth through the air. At each one of his giant steps, the mob, murmuring raucously, fell back even further. Some were already running away between the fires, where the great pieces of carved oak furniture were going up in smoke. The women who formed part of the rabble screamed that he was the Devil incarnate — as more than one cattle prod exploded into pieces with each swing of his iron bars.

Back, back, always backwards moved the mob, retreating now across the courtyards, stumbling over the people they had killed and tumbling into the bonfires they had set. When they finally reached the outer wall, they turned their backs to Christopher and fled. At that moment, and with a final, terrible roar that resounded all over the region, Christopher once again attacked the mob, which, now utterly terror stricken, blew through the open gate, leaped across the drawbridge, and raced, pell-mell down the hill, not stopping until it reached the valley below, where carts were waiting. And Christopher, also crossing over the bridge, stood, immobile and like a great tower, in the middle of the hilltop leaning on his iron bars and wiping the sweat off his forehead. But then, from out of the agitated multitude down below, an old man, bearing no arms, began to come forward. With an olive branch in his hand, he approached Christopher. Halfway up the hill, he stopped. Raising his arms, he asked Christopher why he, a serf, had attacked them, also serfs? He who most certainly must also have suffered from forced servitude, why had he fought against those who, having suffered for so long, only wanted to share in some of the fruits of their labor and of the earth? It was not merely because of a desire to do harm that they had attacked the castles. It was because it was there, inside those walls, that vain, prideful people had enslaved them, and caused their children to suffer hunger and cold homes and them to endure nameless, endless exhaustion. They'd risen up simply to rid the earth of such evils. He, the old man who now spoke this way to Christopher, had worked for fifty years on his piece of land, he'd had his flesh shredded by whips, and he'd seen his home burnt down by the lord and master. All around him, many years before, he'd listened to his children crying out in hunger and watched them shiver in the cold — and then, pushed beyond endurable limits, driven out of his home, trod upon, squeezed and twisted by brute force, and finally thrown away, discarded like some dirty rag, he had picked up a knife and set out to do justice in this world. Out of his entire family, the only person left had been a grandson, a dear little grandson who was six years old and as innocent and simple as an angel. And because the boy had taken an apple from the castle's apple orchard, where he labored as a servant, the master had ordered that the dogs be set on him, that he be left, completely naked, under the snow for one entire winter's night, and that he then be hung by his wrists from a tree. When they cut him down from the tree, he was dying. And the old man's voice trembled. Christopher had let his iron bars drop to the ground, and with his great hands now empty and unsure and open to the free air, and with his head bowed down, he seemed, from the depths of his simplicity, to be thinking about what he had heard. And the old man, moving toward him, asked him if he would now come with them to bring down those monsters who, residing in their black castles, murdered children and if he would help them put an end to those cruel masters, so that under Heaven there could finally be a time, even a short time, when the poor and humble of this earth could breathe freely and wipe their tears away.

And the old man wiped away his tears with his poor, trembling hands. It was at that point that, very slowly and deliberately, Christopher again picked up an iron bar. Little by little, he descended the hill. And the old man, going down in front of him and stumbling along amongst the stones, was shouting so much to his cohorts that it caused the tree branches to rustle: "This is the great giant who is going to set us free!"

The Jacques below scarcely understood him. Some of them, seeing Christopher come down the hill, again fled, leaping over the surrounding walls and ditches. Others, still furious, once again readied their cattle prods. But Christopher, brandishing his iron bar once more, shouted to them, "Follow me!"

And, responding to an irresistible impulse, the entire band of insurrectionists, in a moment of great acclamation, then fell in behind him — and all the while, from high up on the castle walls, the intendant, standing on the battlement among other men of arms, reached out and pointed at Christopher, who had just joined up with the Jacques and, now in their company, was departing across the open plains.

For many days, they made a hard march over hard ground. And it was the old man who guided them. Christopher, walking in silence at his side, carried his iron bar on his shoulder. Behind them came a long line of ragged, tattered men, whose bits and pieces of armor and mail were broken and coming apart. There were battered shields, into which some had stuck plumes, there were naked legs and rough hands holding scythes, cattle prods, and stanchions. After them, came the women, some with skinny children hanging from their skirts, others with babes clutched to their breasts, and the oldest ones bent down under the weight of their burdens, which contained all that they had, a meager bit of bread, some oil, a piece of salted beef. . . . And further back yet came another line of people, old men, shepherds with their crooks and their dogs, reapers, holding their scythes on high, and fugitive serfs, servants, and beggars . . . a long line of poor, miserable people who, because they were starving, could no longer march quickly and who could do no more than leave a long cloud of dust suspended in the still air.

By the early afternoon, and still guided by the old man, they suddenly found themselves, after curving around a grove of pine trees, in front of a great castle, flanked by its two towers. At that very moment, and from over the drawbridge, there came a man on horseback, a gentleman with a long, white beard. He was unarmed. At his side, and riding a hackney horse, there also came forward a governess holding a little girl in her lap. And behind them came four squires armed with lances. Upon seeing, suddenly, that the rabble were still advancing on the castle, the gentleman pulled his horse up short and one of the squires then desperately blew his horn, to which additional bugle calls responded from up on the battlements. And, abruptly turning her mare around, the governess galloped back into the castle. At that point, the castle walls became covered with soldiers. But the unarmed gentleman stayed where he was, without moving, his eagle eyes fixed on the immense crowd of wretched, ragged people that was stretching out in a long line in front of him. From some of them, brandishing their weapons, cries urging them to attack could be heard. When he heard this, Christopher, with a grand gesture of his iron bar, called for silence, and the people quieted down. And, tossing his weapon aside, Christopher then stepped forward, alone and with his arms wide open, toward the gentleman, who sat perfectly still astride his great steed. Up high, the castle walls were now entirely covered with halberdiers and other armed men; down below, the road was black, entirely covered with the wretched of the earth. And then, on the drawbridge, the lord and master of the castle and the giant met, face to face.

In a voice torn, seemingly, from out of the depths of his great chest, Christopher spoke: "We come in peace. We bring our women and children with us. We hold nothing against you . . . But all these people who follow me are hungry. Behind your walls are treasures, bins full of bread, great pieces of meat roasting in the fires of your hearths. . . . These people, the ones you see with me here, have nothing, not a single copper coin to buy something with. They've labored their entire lives, and yet they suffer from hunger, they see their little children forced to eat the roots of plants, and then they die, off in some remote corner of the forest, like wild animals. For them, life is a constant torment. . . . Share what you have with these poor people here before you, as an act of alms giving. Share with them some of your abundance. If you wish, come with me and we will pass among them. Do not be afraid. Walk with me through this multitude, look at their poor, emaciated bodies, see the little children crying from hunger, the old women staggering under their loads. . . . They live in total misery, and they can suffer no more. . . . Take pity on them!"

Having spoken in this fashion, Christopher reverted back into his simplicity and once again became mute, and, with the great, stupid eyes of a beast of burden, he stared, fixedly, at the castle. Slowly, and with a touch of the reins, the feudal lord, pensive and with his head down, then turned his horse around and, still without haste, disappeared back through the castle door. But the doors did not close. And, before long, a servant leading a cow emerged from inside the castle. Others then came out bearing sheep, while still other servants brought strong wicker baskets full of bread and sacks of beans. And others came bearing chests full of money and treasure. And once they'd collected it all in a pile in front of the drawbridge, one of the servants shouted, as he retired back into the castle, "Here is the gift from my lord and master to these poor people who are passing through!"

The drawbridge was then raised up with a great clanking of iron chains.

At the command of the old man, the Jacques began, in an orderly fashion, to pack up onto their shoulders and to fill their carts with the gifts given them by the seigneur. And then, once again, they set out on the road, but with Christopher, still bearing his iron bar and seemingly so astonished by this that he was unable to speak, now leading them.

As they were passing through the foothills of a nearby mount, they came across a bubbling brook. And there the Jacques stopped and made camp for the night. Very quickly, campfires were lit. The old man posted sentries at all four corners of the encampment. And that night the children did not cry out in hunger, and there was a sense of gratitude in the hearts of the people. Christopher wanted only a small piece of bread. He drank from the pure water of the brook — and, as the Jacques slept, stretched out on the ground under the trees, he, seated on a rock, gazed up at the stars and thought about Jesus, who, he felt, was behind them, and by the light of his starry lamps Christopher thought he saw him, there, among the most wretched of his world, like a father among his children.

In the morning, the Jacques broke camp, gathered up their things, and, guided as always by the old man and by the friar, departed, following the stream until, arriving at the first oak trees of a great forest, they smelled a nauseating stench. And then they saw a man, a serf, hanging from the branch of a tree. His body had been half eaten away by crows. When some of the Jacques, who'd gone on ahead, found more bodies hanging from trees, a sense of indignation ran through the Jacques. As the people began to shout and cry out, the crows were frightened away, fleeing into the tree branches. And underneath the feet of the dead men, still hanging there on ropes, the ground was covered with the tracks of wolves. Up on high, on top of a hill, the towers of a castle, black in the clear light of a new day, could be seen. And what Christopher and his people were staring at here had to be the justice of the lord who lived there.

At that point, a wave of anger swept over the Jacques. Some wanted to immediately set fire to the forest so that the castle would be swept up in the conflagration. Others spoke of cutting down trees to make battering rams they could use to knock down the castle walls. Suddenly, Christopher, stepping around the moss-covered rocks that covered it and urged forward by the people who, behind him, were brandishing their scythes and cattle prods, headed up the road that led to the castle. Then, the mob caught sight of a tower standing off to the side of the castle. It was the prison where people were kept under house arrest, and it was flanked by tall walls, black and somber but, because of the new stones that had been added, splotched with white, as if they were siege scars. The drawbridge was drawn up and an iron grating had fallen down in front of it. A palisade of heavy beams encircled the greenish waters of the moat. Not a sound emanated from the castle walls. Everything gave the impression of having been abandoned. On one side, huge boulders had come crashing down and remained in disorder. An eagle soared high overhead.

A sense of unease fell over the Jacques as they confronted that sinister silence. Some, thinking the castle to be abandoned, argued that they should pass it by and continue on. Others said they should scale its walls and take it. Christopher, without any apparent plan, stepped forward toward the drawbridge. Suddenly, and with the clanging of iron chains, the drawbridge came down, and from out of the castle doors, which had been flung open, a troop of knights burst out at a gallop, with their visors down, their lances at the ready, and their armor clanking. The Jacques recoiled, en masse. Christopher stood, alone, on the open ground.

At the front of the knights, one of them, with great, white plumes attached to his helmet and his lance poised for attack, came charging at Christopher, who was without his iron bar.

Instead, he ran to a pine tree and, laying hold of it with both hands, tore it from the ground. Grabbing it as if it were a giant broom, he wielded it, just as a servant sweeps a floor, against the onrushing knight and his horse, both of whom came crashing down, in a great tangle of animal and arms, in the dense foliage. Leaping forward, Christopher grabbed the knight and, restraining him between his knees as if he were a powerless infant, undid the buckles of his helmet and uncovered a human face, one livid and covered with a thick red beard. Then, hoisting him up into the air and using him like a shield against the other knights, who, in mute terror, had now come to a halt, Christopher, seeing the desperate situation they were in, bellowed out, "A ransom! A ransom!" The Jacques, wanting to smash to pieces the lord he'd taken prisoner, encircled Christopher. But instead Christopher held up even higher the poor knight, who was not moving, for all to see, and once again cried out, "A ransom! A ransom!"

The other knights, now reanimated, threw themselves at him. But Christopher, leaping to the edge of a rocky crag and bending the man over as if he were going to cast him down into the rocks and waters of the abyss below, shouted out once more, "A ransom!" This time, the opposing knights stopped and quickly began, with great gestures from their iron gloves, to consult each other, until, finally, one of them stepped forward and said, "Very well. He is ransomed."

The old man then approached and explained the terms of the ransom. He wanted money, twenty sacks of bread, cattle, and wine to sustain his people and two carts to haul it in. But he also wanted them to swear a solemn oath, on a cross, that his band would not be pursued. The old lord and master reached out and, gripping the friar's cross, swore it.

The Jacques, laying down their arms, then waited — while Christopher, once again seated on a rock and still holding the hapless knight firmly lodged over his knees, and with his right hand gripping his legs and his left hand firmly around his neck, also waited — for the goods to be delivered. Little by little, the servants came and went from the castle bringing out the ransom until it was all there. And then the Jacques proceeded down the road, herding the cattle along and with the two carts with their sacks of bread, the gold, and the wineskins. Only Christopher, still holding the captured knight, remained behind. When the last of his people had disappeared behind the hill, he carefully placed the knight back on the ground, and murmured, in his simple way, "Go!"

And then, without turning around, Christopher strode off to stand once again with the Jacquerie ranks.

There then began, across the provinces and from castle to castle, the march of the Jacques. From out of the villages through which they passed, the miserable ones, the insurgent serfs, the beggars, the poor and hungry of the earth joined up with them. They were now an immense multitude that filled the roads and pathways. But among them, there was neither violence nor rage. To the contrary, they were showing, in one rich baronial estate after another, only the wretchedness and misery of what they were, servants, maids, and serfs, and, with not the slightest sign of violence or rancor, they would beg for alms and bits of charity. Christopher was like a great, loving father who, in the company of his children, was not above asking for help as they traveled along the roadways. When they would appear before a castle, they would show their ragged and tattered clothes, their emaciated faces, and the scars of their bondage, and they would cry out for bread. The doors, making a great racket, would then open and people, some motivated by pity while others perhaps more motivated by fear, would dip into their coffers and granaries and give them something. Day and night, Christopher maintained order in his immense throng of people. He did not permit anyone to strip the trees of their fruit or steal the cattle from their pastures. The only thing that was acceptable was to take the charity that was offered them. If he and his people came across beggars or famished clowns and circus performers, he would shout to them, "Come. Join us." His great heart made him take upon himself all human suffering and shelter all the miserable men, women, and children of the earth and to go with them as they begged for alms and charity along the roads and byways of the world. When he received money from people, he would distribute it among the poorest villages. When the children ran up to him with their empty sacks, he would, in great handfuls, fill them up with grain and beans. A new sense of kindness and mercy was taking root in the miserable beings of his rag-tag band. Some of them had thrown away their scythes. Others, when they passed by small country churches or lone crosses, would fall on their knees, sobbing.

And always, now, Christopher was out in front, leading them like a great human tower marching along and moving forward. Their adoration washed over him. "Our giant is a saint," they would say. And, in their newfound confidence, they felt life would be like this forever, a long march along roadways in which they would gather up the goods and wealth that the nobles wanted to share with the poor. Surely this would be a sign that Jesus had returned to earth. Surely it would not now be long before all the castles opened themselves up, before they shared their riches, and before they destroyed their arms. There would never again be famine or war and, in their stead, there would reign, in the sweet peace of the countryside, a brotherhood of man in which everyone was well provisioned and cared for. Their encampment, when they stopped to rest, was like a village at feast time, one where the meat on the spits was plentiful and where every hand held a thick slice of bread. Their long, hard march was now moderating, and sometimes its people, in a happy repose and having forgotten the miseries of their lives, would stay for a time in some valley or along the banks of a gurgling stream. Among the women and children who'd chosen to remain in the nearby villages, there was no longer any anxiety — because each and every day messengers were sent out to their hovels bearing money and provisions. Some people in Christopher's band, however, the ones who had already saved something up for their nest eggs, now returned, with no fear, to their distant former homes. Such was their confidence in Jesus.

And through it all, Christopher felt an enormous happiness. Day and night, he stood vigilant over the enormous mob of poor people so that no form of violence or brutish behavior could erupt in it. Of the issues and conflicts that did come up, he resolved them by extending his arms and reaching out to the people. If someone stole fruit along the way, he or she was expelled from the group. Christopher's justice was applied equally to everyone. And to everyone he also gave his charity. And it was he, and no one else, who removed the thorns from injured feet and who helped the old people who were too tired and worn out from their march to go on.

Thus did they wander through the open countryside, until, one afternoon, as they were nearing a great lake, one that, edged with canebrakes, sparkled brilliantly in the October sun, they saw on the other side a large troop of knights, whose pennants were trembling in the air. Working their separate ways around the lake, the two groups would certainly encounter each other — which, in a short time, they did. Surprised, both the Jacques and the knights came to a halt, each regarding the other warily.

Lying between them was a great open plain, one full of flowers and covered with green plants now turning an October yellow and stretching off to a line of hills dressed in pine forests. The sun was sparkling brilliantly on the waters of the lake — and then a vast silence fell over it all.

At the front of the weaponless Jacques, a concerned Christopher had decided what he would do — and so he started to stride forward, straight toward the knights. On behalf of his poor people, he would ask for their charity. Suddenly, from behind him, his minions began to shout, "Stop! Stop!" The men of arms, having deployed into a long battle line, suddenly charged at the miserable crowd, their lances leveled directly at them. With a cry, the old man ordered his people to grab up their cattle prods, their scythes, and their lances and to form a wall of iron against the black and iron-clad heavy cavalry galloping at them and making the ground shake. As they were thundering down upon him, Christopher could hear the puffing and snorting of the horses.

Suddenly, there was a terrible crash as the confused mass of iron fell upon the Jacques, followed by a ferocious clash of arms as the furious blows of the riders' broadswords and the breastplates of their spurred-on chargers carved out huge furrows among the Jacques, who fell, run through by lances and decapitated by the great, quivering blades being wielded in such lethal two-handed fashion against them. The Jacquerie legions had been split in two — with a huge gap in between them that was covered in bodies, now being trampled on by the hoofs of the enormous warhorses. Then, as these two divisions were running to attack the troop of knights, this group itself split into two units to face the two attacking Jacquerie forces, and the entire plain was filled with the crash and clamor of two great battles. Peons and mounted knights, now thrown together in a bloody tangle of crashing steel and anguished cries where the prods of the Jacques shattered against armor and swords and the long, steel-spurred cudgels of the knights crushed craniums protected, sometimes, by nothing more than an ancient iron morion. The trumpets of the knights blared furiously. Lightning-like flashes of steel filled the air amongst the fluttering of elegant helmeted plumes.

The Jacques, having seen their pathetic weapons smashed to pieces, threw themselves upon the necks and withers of the horses and, in their collective strength, knocked off their mounts several knights, who, tumbling down to the ground in a terrible crash of weapons and armor, then disappeared under a storm of arms and hands armed with knives. Other

Jacques, carrying scythes, opened up the bellies of the horses. Some of the knights, now on foot and fighting on the ground, were swinging their swords in great circles — and the stones that the Jacques hurled at them clanked furiously against the metal of their breastplates. Four huge reapers, moving along slowly, as if they were passing through a field of ripe corn stalks, worked their way forward through the melee, swinging their scythes in a regular motion and severing the hamstrings of the horses, lopping off arms which were being detached from their iron guards, and slicing through the throats of their helmetless enemies. And in the midst of the combat, an enormous and disheveled Christopher, weaponless and like someone not wishing to shed blood, strode through the battlefield with his enormous arms yanking knights from off their saddles and throwing them to the ground, like bundles of rusty metal. Blood was running down his face and chest and across his leather kilt, which had been torn to shreds. His tremendous bellowing caused the horses to rear up in fear. Laying hold of the knights' broadswords, he broke them like straws. The steel-tipped clubs and shields that he ripped away from them went flying, like leaves carried off by a blast of wind. Sometimes running, with his two arms outstretched and his fists, which were bigger than a ram's head, he knocked to the ground, with a dry thud, both knights and their horses. But then, stepping into a pile of ropes, he became entangled. The mountain of rope trapped him, and when he pulled at one of the cords, he caused the rest to ensnare him even more. His legs became caught in a hard knot and he was thrown to the ground, like a steer in the marketplace. Little by little, all the knights now converged on him. Struggling to his feet once again, though weaponless, Christopher's feet stumbled against a dead body covered in armor. Snatching up the cadaver, he used it as he would a cudgel. Christopher then began to fall back, toward the highest of the pine-covered hills. Arrows were falling all around him; rocks thrown by his attackers were crashing against him. The giant drew back even more — until, suddenly, he counterattacked! Charging directly at his assailants, Christopher knocked one down and laid out another with great blows from the dead body, which, by now, had lost its helmet. The circle of knights that hemmed him in was growing ever larger. Shouting insults at him, its members, still at a distance, drew close enough to strike him with their steel-tipped clubs. And with every attack, the circle around him grew tighter and tighter. And it bristled with glinting iron weapons. Serene, Christopher whirled around and around his cadaver, whose armor was now breaking up, piece by piece, retaining, finally, nothing more than the leg cuisses by which Christopher was holding him. Clear for all to see were the dead man's white flesh and the stiff hair of his chest. But from taking such a battering, finally, the man's body was fast losing the strength of flesh and bone that had held it together. Its cranium was crushed, its arms were now soft and floppy, like rags, and its chest was shattered — and its formerly terrible right arm, now in the control of Christopher, was nothing more than a strip of soft flesh. Finally, Christopher reached the hilltop. There, thanks to each and every pine tree, he had a potential weapon. Turning around, he laid his hands on an enormous tree trunk, intending to tear it, roots and all, from out of the ground. Suddenly, however, an arrow pierced Christopher's knee. It felled him for a moment, and caused him to slide down a moist and slick incline of the hill. Then, in an instant, a great black courser passed over him and he saw the flash of a lance. . . . Christopher lay prostrate on the ground, completely motionless, and with bloody spume in his mouth.

The knights were closing in on him when a great clamor surged up behind them. It was the Jacques, who had now regrouped and, led forward by the friar, were attacking that group of knights who found themselves trapped between the hillside and the soft ground where the horses' hoofs would sink in. Realizing this, the lancers turned their horses and fled, galloping off between the hill, strewn with dead bodies, and the onrushing Jacques, who, once again, occupied the flat, open ground. Bellowing in defiance at the fleeing knights, the Jacques pursued them on foot and launched their remaining arrows at them. Then, and in a torrent of derisive gestures and insults, they hurled handfuls of thick, slimy mud at them. But, upon seeing the peons thus exposed on the open ground, the knights pulled up abruptly, did a turnabout, and attacked the miserable ones. It was a terrible killing field. The friar fell first, his head split open and with his cross clutched tightly in his hand. Those that tried to escape were hunted down everywhere and, once they'd been driven to the lake's edge, great lances forced them to disappear under its waters.

Now, on the vast plain, there were only men of arms. The Jacques were strewn about, lying in pools of black blood. Astride their horses and trotting along, slowly, among them, the knights finished off the wounded and the dying, who cried out from thirst. Other knights, having done their business, removed their shields and wiped off great drops of sweat. The physicians bound up their wounded limbs. And the pages brought them great tankards of wine. The sun was going down, and the lake, behind its black canebrakes, had taken on a golden sheen. A flock of wild ducks flew overhead, in the now pale sky. And, at the trumpet's call, the scattered noblemen came together again, reforming their ranks. Their wounded were placed in wagons. And then, slowly, the troop of knights headed back to their castle by the path that led around the lake, where, by now, the luster of gold had been extinguished by the night, and leaving it utterly black and sad.

/ / /

On the vast, open field, the Jacques lay dead. Their grand march, which had carried to the castles and abbeys what, to the people in them, seemed a strange and alien vision of the miseries and multitudes of the earth, had come to an end. None of them would ever return to their villages and their hovels, where their children waited for them, late into the night, beside their cold, fireless hearths. The Jacques were dead, and the land would be wiped clean of their rags.

Christopher lay, outstretched, up on the hill, among the pine trees. A cold, sad wind passed over him. He opens his eyes and, with great difficulty, gets up on his hands and knees and gazes out at the scene before him on the plain. And as far as he can see, in any direction, there is nothing but piles of dead bodies, between which the eyes of the wolves are already gleaming. The great lake is still. Overhead, the full moon is passing. An immense pain chills his heart. Once again, his eyes close — and he collapses on the ground, seemingly lifeless.

All night long, however, he relived the battle. From out of the mountains of dead Jacques other Jacques began to rise up, with other uniforms and other arms, and impelled to revolt once again because of the same misery that had oppressed the earlier ones. And always from out of the depths of the horizon, and from the heights of the mountains, from their very tops, there would descend on them mounted knights who bore different arms, who shouted different war cries at them, and who charged at the Jacques, smashing them and again leaving them for dead beneath the full moon. But then, from out of these same dead Jacques, still others would emerge, this time more pale, and only little by little, but brandishing now the pickaxes of the miners and the tools of the workshops, and, flaunting their rags and starving children, they were once again demanding justice. Just as quickly, though, and on the order of a bellow coming from up on high, powerful squadrons began to descend upon them, squadrons of armed men led by robed magistrates and men carrying sacks of gold, and who once again fell upon the Jacques and laid them low, prostrate and lifeless on some mountain or plain that the moon, paler and waning now, covered in a milky white light and a profound silence. And so it was that in this fashion, and without the limitation of either time or place, living Jacques were eternally reborn from the bones of the dead Jacques and becoming on each occasion more numerous until, finally, the open plain they were on here had become a bramble of emaciated arms clamoring for, pleading for, and demanding equality. And immediately other manorial squadrons would descend upon them, this time, however, greatly diminished in numbers and with an attack that was less determined and more hesitant and that struck ever more feeble blows. Until, finally, and at long last, the Jacques were so innumerable that they extended from the plains to the mountains, and the moon, which was casting its still pale, waning light on everything there, clearly illuminated multitudes that were disciplined, armed, and aware, and that were advancing with order and rhythm. The squadrons moving against this band of cohorts now melted away, like wax before a flame. The Jacques now occupied the entire earth. One final, lone knight approached them and, realizing that he and his were defeated, laid down his arms and disappeared. And so, finally, the earth knew only the Jacques, who now sang songs of triumph in the fresh, clear morning air.

Then, feeling on his face this freshness, Christopher opened his eyes, which were still uncertain and half asleep, as in a dream. The pure, cool light of the morning penetrated through the boughs that covered him. The birds were singing brightly in their nests, and with rustling wings they flitted from one branch to another. The sweet fragrance of lavender and fresh green plants perfumed the air. And in the still humid grass, lustrous in the morning dew, there were wildflowers, buttercups, and poppies everywhere. A trickle of cold water ran singing its way between the rocks. And it seemed to Christopher that, at that moment, he was seeing off in the distance a boy, with long blond hair and wearing a white tunic that was covered by the folds of a white cloak, emerge from among the boughs and pine trees and, leaning on a white staff, come toward him. His steps, no heavier than the linen of his clothing, were so light that the poppies were not even bent down as he, white and airy, passed over them, giving off a delicious aroma as sweet as the blossoming in that soil of flowers not of this earth. He drew nearer and nearer — and Christopher could see that his eyes, which shone like two evening stars, were fixed on him. Gently, he kneeled down at Christopher's side, laying down his staff so lightly that it did not even depress the fine tips of the green plants beneath it. Then, and with fingers softer than velvet, he let them play over Christopher's wounds. Immediately, Christopher sensed that all his pain had disappeared and that a new strength was coursing through him. The boy then tore off a strip from his mantel and, dividing it in two, placed one piece on Christopher's leg wound and the other on his chest wound. To Christopher, those strips of linen felt as light as the air and as sweet smelling as jasmine. After doing this, the boy picked up his white staff and left, in silence. He penetrated deep into the forest and, little by little, was lost from sight among the dark tree trunks, which, for a moment afterwards, retained the bright clarity of that white passage. The birds began once again to sing. The branches recommenced their soft swaying in the breeze. Christopher moved his arms — and then raised up his enormous body. All of his wounds were healed. And, feeling a new strength, that good giant headed off through the pine forest — and began, once again, to traverse the world.

XV/

Christopher journeyed to faraway lands. And through all the places and cities he traveled, he sought, in the simplicity of his heart, only to be of service and to do good. He would knock at the doors of huts and hovels and ask if there were needed two strong arms there for any and all work. He never asked to be paid. A tiny crust of bread was sufficient for him. For water, he drank from the freshest brooks. No labor, no matter how much effort it required or how loathsome it might be, ever troubled him. He cleaned up waste and filth and vermin with pious care, and he always asked for the heaviest load. He took the ax from the woodcutters' hands and cut down the forests. He pulled the boats with tow ropes. He hitched himself to the tongues of the wagons. And if a countryman wanted to send his donkey to church to be blessed or freed from all evil, he, Christopher, would hoist the animal up to his shoulders and carry it along with as much care as if he were bearing a maiden. If people hurt him, he would humbly lower his face. If they beat him, he would stand perfectly still under the blows. If they dismissed him, he would pick up his walking stick and, sighing, simply go away.

Out on the road, he would sit down at crossroads so he could guide pilgrims, travelers, and circus performers on their way. If there were some great quagmire, he would position himself at the edge of it and ferry, on his back, both men and their animals across it. He was the one who broke the rocks so that roads could be built. And in the forests, he was the one who knew the paths the merchant caravans should follow, and it was he who would build great bonfires to drive away the wild boars.

Occasionally, he would consent to serve one master only. Thus it was that he once became the servant of a self-proclaimed healer, and he was expected to pull, like a mule, the man's giant carriage in which the wide-mouthed pots and jugs, containing herbs and unguents, clinked and clanked together and which, every afternoon, would stop in the churchyards after mass. But, sensing that the quack was both self-centered and mean-spirited, he soon left his service. After that, he was the squire for a knight errant, whom he came upon sitting on the edge of a fountain and bathing a wound he'd received in his leg. Christopher bound up his wound and began to follow him on his adventures, walking along behind both him and his charger and carrying a large club he'd made from a pine tree. With the knight, he performed many great deeds. He freed the servants of a harsh master who had hanged some of them for not having taken off their caps as he passed them on the road; he chased away the robbers and highwaymen who infested the forests; and he returned to an orphan the earldom that had been stolen from him by avaricious relatives. But, as the knight, having once helped save a damsel in distress, and whom he later came to marry, thereby gaining a manorial estate, had abandoned the road and its life of adventure, Christopher, not wishing to live in idleness, also left the service of that good knight, taking with him, as a form of payment, a sack full of gold and good, warm clothing, all of which he immediately distributed among the poor.

From then on, and following the example of the knight, Christopher set himself to helping the oppressed. At night, as he passed by the castles, he would knock down the gallows. If he knew of a camp or settlement that had been sacked, he would force the thief to make restitution. He would save the bands of merchants from being assaulted by the lords and nobles who, with their great lances, would attack them on the roads and rob them. Wherever he might learn of some lord who had imposed an excessive amount of labor on his servants, he, and no one else, would go there and perform the work. And not even once, in his presence, would he allow a little child to be punished. If he passed by a dwelling where there was a woman crying and a rumor of her having been beaten, he would take the stick from out of the hands of the husband. And when soldiers were supposed to pass through a village, he would be there, on guard, to prevent them from doing cruel, unjust things. And no one dared to affront or defy him.

But Christopher was growing old. His hair had become coarse, uneven, and bristly. He had only rags to cover his body, and his beard was wild and overgrown, like thick underbrush. And the incomparable kindness of his gaze and of his smile were hidden, rendered invisible, underneath his beard and bushy eyebrows — and for those who saw him, his appearance, in truth, was horrible and frightening.

When Christopher would enter into a city, the children would flee from him and all the doors would be slammed shut in his face. And the men standing guard would inquire as to where he had come from, what barony he belonged to, and if he had permission to wander along the roadways. His response was always that he wanted only to work. And so, quietly and humbly, would he wait, next to a fountain or in the corner of some square, hoping that very soon these doors would open up to him, and that, now smiling, the children would come around. They all reminded Christopher of the Joana of his village. By this time, she must have become a woman. And perhaps, and in her turn, she too now had, hanging onto her skirts, a little girl, one as blond and as gracious as she had been. He would call over to him some of the still frightened children and have them jump over his knees. And from the latticework windows, their mothers smiled. Now, no one feared the giant — and he, feeling accepted, immediately began to help the brick-layers as they would put up houses, or he would push out a cart that had become stuck in the mud. Soon, everyone wanted the help of that immense powerhouse. And he was the one who cleaned up the mar-kets, who whitewashed the towers with fresh coats of paint, who trans-ported the bundles, who cleared the snow and ice from off the rivers during the winter, who watered down the dusty roads during the sum-mers, who repaired the roofs, who put out the fires, and — seating him-self at the door of the hospitals — who took it upon himself to bury the poor when they died. Pressing his face against the high bars of the prison walls, he consoled the prisoners, assisted the ones who were con-demned to hard labor, and, collecting his salary in bread or hard cash, Christopher, sitting down in a churchyard, would then distribute it to the beggars.

Finally, one day, as he was departing from a city, he met, out on the road, a poor circus performer with one wooden leg and accompanying a sick woman who had an infant suckling at her breast. They were so miserable and sad — he, with a sword under his arm, and she with a sack suspended from her shoulders that contained large and small juggling balls — that Christopher began to trudge down the road with them. Along the way, he found out that, in another time, they'd traveled the roads and paths and worked the fairs, making a decent living and (ever since he, in a fall, had lost his leg) showing their trained dogs and a monkey that performed amazing tricks.

A few days earlier, however, when they were resting for a time in a roadside tavern some men came in, the squires and armed soldiers of a local nobleman. After a time, they'd gotten drunk and there was an altercation, the result of which was, in a flurry of saber blows, that they killed the monkey and the poor dogs. With them gone, the couple's ability to make a living was gone, too. He, the man, could not work because he was lame. And now, the only thing that was left for them was a life of begging, until one day the cold and hunger would lay out the three of them — even the child — prostrate and dead along the side of some road. And then, the circus mountebank added, "Blessed and happy are you, whom God made so huge that you can exhibit yourself at the fairs and make more money than a lettered person can by writing!" Clearly, the mountebank had taken him, Christopher, for one of those giants who get shown off at the fairs. And, with this thought having scarcely passed through his mind, Christopher, in his simplicity, proposed to him that, in exchange for bread and half the profits, he take Christopher to a fair and exhibit him in a tent. The poor mountebank all but cried from happiness at hearing this, and straight away they all headed off in the direction of a big fair that, every year and in honor of Saint Michael, was held next to a large walled city.

They arrived during the night and, once they'd obtained permission from the guards to go in, the mountebank went immediately to see one of those Jews who lent money. He asked for a loan, which he needed to set up a stall, to erect a platform, to hang red canvas curtains, and to secure a drum they would use to promote the giant. The Jew, after he'd examined Christopher carefully and determined that his appearance was, indeed, that of a proper monster and that it would result in a good revenue, counted out, one by one, ten pieces of silver into the mountebank's hand. And then, after he'd signed the paper in front of the fair's superintendent, the mountebank left with Christopher to build the stall. All night long the two of them worked, hammering and nailing, while the clown's wife hurriedly sewed a scarlet tunic for Christopher to wear.

By the next day, everything was ready, including the large banner of white cloth that, held up by two large posts, announced the world's greatest giant and the great defender of Navarre and of the world. Christopher, inside the tent and sitting on a large, carpet-covered chest, waited, while outside the mountebank, beating on his drum, stirred up interest in the marvelous wonder he had inside. His wife, wearing, in the manner of a Moorish woman, metal sequins in her long, tangled braids, stood at the front of the tent with a copper plate, into which the tickets were to be dropped.

The fair was enormous, spreading out over a vast meadow that fronted up against the walls of the city. The tents and stalls, made of canvas, wood, rugs, and even tree branches, were lined up so as to form great streets and pathways. On the tops of the poles, streamers and pennants fluttered in the breeze. And men, decked out like Orientals, and women, some with great plumes in their hair and others wearing clothes from strange, unknown countries, would congregate behind the counters, where, depending on the street and the particular proprietors therein, they would find great bales of fine fabric waiting to be unrolled for them, jewels, resplendent in their grilled boxes and beckoning to them, exotic essences of perfumes lined up for their perusal, and mountains of furs, all mixed up with fine, inlaid arms. On other streets, and under canvas tents, were cooking fires and food stands and great casks of beer and wine. The mountebanks occupied a spot near the river that was covered in shade by tall elm trees. And all around them, and covering the entire vast plain, was a confusion of unloaded carts, piles of wood, herds of horses tied up at the hoof, and great wicker baskets in which birds thrashed about.

Scarcely had the doors of the city been opened when the people began to fill the fair's alleys and streets, the green plants of which began to fast disappear under their feet. And very soon the air was filled with the cries of the street vendors, the shouts of the barkers calling out to their customers, the sounds of the kettledrums being played at the doors of the taverns, and the ringing of little bells.

But no one made a greater racket than the lame mountebank, who banged away desperately on his drum in front of the tent where that good giant waited, pensively. It wasn't long before men from the town, women leading children by the hand, fair-goers, and even other hawkers began to come in, dropping, as they did so, a silver coin in the broad copper plate. And no sooner had the curtain been raised than a long, slow, and amazed "Ah . . . !" came from the lips of the audience. The booth had been built tall, in the form of a tower, and Christopher — now revealed up on the stage and dressed in a long, scarlet tunic bordered with spangles, paillettes, and tinsel, wearing a turban from which enormous green plumes waved about, and carrying a colossal wooden scimitar under his yellow waistband — was, in truth, a frightful creature to behold, like one of the misshapen ogres told about in fairy tales. Full of timidity, Christopher did not move his arms. And a great sense of shame began to come over him as he stood before those astonished faces, which were filled with fear at his great size and strength and with something like pity at his deformity. The children hid themselves in their mothers' skirts — and the men, dumbfounded, wanted to feel the firmness of his muscles. Each group that came to gawk at Christopher would later go into the taverns telling tales and spreading stories about the marvels of that giant. Myths and legends began to grow and circulate — it was he, and no one else, who'd defeated the emperor of Occitania, it was he who'd slain a terrible dragon that had infested the Algarves, and it was he who, merely by pushing it, had knocked down the tower erected by the Devil for Robert of Normandy. All day long there was a long line waiting at the entrance of their stall — and at night, it was said, the mountain of money that had piled up in the copper plate would turn to dust.

Little by little, Christopher had grown accustomed to the crowds — and, in order to make the children laugh, he would sometimes grimace or scowl or he would take hold of a man by his legs and lift him high into the air, as if he weighed no more than a piece of straw. Later, he might use two fingers to hoist up a barrel full of stones, he might bend thick iron bars with his teeth, or he might, with a single blow of his clenched fist, split a millstone in two.

At night, he was covered in sweat. And while the mountebank and his wife, their faces radiant, would gather their money together in piles, he would gather to his breast and gently rock the little child, who, cradled in his arms, would always enjoy a sweet sleep.

Soon, Christopher's fame had spread throughout the town. And even the prince who there reigned, along with the bishop himself, came, accompanied by their great entourage of knights and pages, to see the giant. A sense of beholding something marvelous enveloped them. And the prince, a man of great musculature, wanted to measure his strength against that of Christopher and to wager to see which of them would bend over the hand of the other. And in the presence of all those knights, and out of a sense of humility, Christopher ceded to the prince and allowed his hairy hand to bend his. The knights cheered their lord and monarch. And the prince, flush with victory, poured out the contents of his gold-filled sack into Christopher's hands, exempted the mountebank's stall from the superintendent's taxes, and ordered that, during the evening, the kitchen servants, carrying torches, bring a leg of venison and meat pies to their table.

Every night, the mountebank, dividing up the day's money, would give Christopher his half, which he then kept in a hole in the ground, off in a corner of their shack and covered by a big millstone. Later in the evening, he would then go out alone through the fair grounds and whatever labor or service there was that needed to be done, he would do it. He carried kegs of wine on his back, he lifted the loads from other people and bore them himself, he cleaned the floors of the other fair stalls and huts, and, at the doors of the kitchens, he would wash the tin plates and cups.

But the end of the fair was finally approaching, and, one night, as he sensed that the level of activity in various stalls was winding down, the mountebank, as always, counted out that day's take. Suddenly, his face was bathed in dancing tears of joy because he realized that, now and for ever more, he was protected from misery and want. At that moment, Christopher dug up his own treasure and, in silence, went over and added it to the mountebank's money, murmuring, "It's for the child." Two copper coins rolled out onto the floor. Christopher picked them up and put them to his lips, as if they were alms that had been tossed his way, kissed the child, and left the shack. And then, buying a piece of cornbread and a mug of wine, he left behind the fair that was coming to its end.

XVI /

Once again, Christopher traveled the world, serving mankind. Through the desolate and uninhabited regions and through places of great habitation, and through the long winters and the long springs, he roamed the world, offering others the strength of his limbs. The years passed, and now Christopher was older than the oldest oaks. His long hair had grown white, and his strength was no longer as great as it once had been. But each day, his heart swelled with a kindness and a tenderness each time greater than the last, yet also vaguer and more all-encompassing. Sometimes, as he was seated on a rock at the edge of a road, Christopher would gaze at the trees, the fields, the mountains, and the simple wildflowers, and at those times he would feel a profound desire to embrace the entire earth and hold it close to his heart. He would then think about how there lived upon that earth so many miserable people, so many who were humble and meek, and so many who were sick and in need of help — and there would come over him a great urge to plumb the deepest, darkest recesses of that world and cure every pain, end every hunger, and make the world happy, healthy, and perfect. He then set off, and as he traveled down different roads, he would beg so that he would have something to give to the people who really had to beg. A living example of succor and support that stood by, always ready to help, he would situate himself around where people entered the bridges, and assist an old person or bear someone's burden. His one desire was that he, and he alone, bear all of humanity's burdens. And sometimes he would stop and look around, as if seeking out, in the vast horizons in front of him, new forms of service to offer people and new weaknesses to bolster. At those moments, he would imagine that uncountable numbers of poor, needy people would quickly and surely present themselves before his eyes. And then he would depart once again, having become sad because during the entire day his powerful arms had remained idle. For what purpose, then, had Jesus given him such strong, powerful limbs? Like a source of strength ready to work and ready to help, Christopher would then go and sit down right at the bridge entrances, where the flow of people was greater. If it was a gentleman or a knight who passed by, he would run and get water for his horse. If it was a drayman, he would help the mules pull the cart. If it was a beggar, he, Christopher, would beg for him.

Little by little, his inherent goodness came to include animals as well. They, too, suffered, and they, too, had, on this earth, their share of misery and of pain. From then on, whenever he saw an animal too heavily loaded, he would take its burden and place it on his own shoulders. He would collect bones, from around the markets and street corners, to distribute among the starving dogs. He was the nurse of hurt and damaged animals, whose fly-infested wounds he would clean and tend. Even a little bird, swooping and diving through the air, filled his breast with kindness, tenderness, and mercy. And he would penetrate deep into the woods in the hope of being able to care for old, sick wolves or deer that were dying because of hunger during the winter snows.

Later on, and from out of the depths of his simple and dense soul, there came little by little to be born the idea that the trees also suffered, as did the little flowers in the fields. And from that time on, Christopher never again carved a shepherd's crook from out of a tree trunk. From that time on, all branches that were dry, broken, and lying on the ground pained him and made him suffer. He would step aside so as not to tread on fresh, green plants. And during the periods of drought, he would make long treks to the river to bring back water he would then give to the plants, suffocating in the dust of the road, so that they, too, would have something to drink. Even rocks and stones, he finally came to suspect, might well be able to feel pain and suffering. The pickax that cut and broke them, the hard wheels that crossed and cracked them, the sun that scalded them, and the cold snow that buried them ... how could these things not cause them pain, a pain they guarded in the profundity of their muteness? And many times, with his vast body, he provided shade for the rocks; and during the periods of cold, his hands, working like long spades, would free these same rocks and stones from the icy frigidity that imprisoned them.

Christopher's kindness and mercy now embraced the entire universe. Sometimes, at night, he would be gazing up at Heaven and feel an intense love for the stars themselves. They were so clear and pure. One moment they were twinkling and shining and the next they were gone.

And the moon, as it came out, was so sad that a soundless sigh lifted itself out of Christopher's heart. Where did they all go, those stars, so fast and so quickly? Finally, he came to think that they must be souls flying upward through the heavenly spaces, ascending higher and higher so that they became purer and purer, gaining a league each day for every act of kindness done, and reaching, finally, a state of perfection such that they would be worthy of being absorbed into the sublime bosom of Jesus.

Thus it was that our good giant grew older. And it came to pass, one day, as he was walking along a line of hills and making his way in between steep rocks, that he thought he heard a murmur of voices that seemed to be coming from the depths of the cliffs and precipices all about him. Christopher climbed down, holding on to the edges of the rocks. And he saw a long river, black and wild, racing along over the big rocks that cut it into channels, kicking up spume and emitting a somber moan. Standing on its bank, he could make out a band of merchants with their heavily laden mules. On the other side, there were steep, rocky crags that gave way to a mountain that quickly rose up from the river and that was crowned by black pine trees.

Christopher came down the mountain and approached the men. Fearful of his size and deformities, they all huddled together and pulled huge knives from out of their belts. After a little time, which Christopher spent speaking with them from a distance and with great humility, the men gradually began to come nearer, asking him what had happened to the bridge that used to be there. Christopher did not know. They then told him that there had been a short, easy path running through there, and throughout those parts, but that there was also that bad part, the wild river. In another, earlier time, there'd been a bridge across it made of small boats tied together with iron chains, but the river's force had broken the chains and carried off the boats like little pieces of dry straw. After that, a new, wooden bridge was built, but the river carried that off, too. In the meantime, the master of those lands had died, and, with the lands passing into the hands of someone else — someone who lived in the city — no one took it upon himself to raise up another bridge for the wayfarers. And now there they all were, unable to get across, and with their wives and children waiting in vain for them in their dwellings beyond the mountains.

All this while, Christopher was staring at the turbulent waters. And then, silently, he waded into the river and began to cross it. The water soon came up to his knees, then to his waist, and then, finally, it beat furiously against his chest, as if he were the great pillar of a new bridge. And Christopher strode on, pressing further and further into the wild river. After a time, Christopher emerged from the water waist high and, a moment later, his knees came into view as well. Finally, and running now, he set foot on the hard rocks of the other side, where a steep, arduous pathway climbed upward into the rocky crags. Christopher had forded the river.

He turned around and, opening his arms out wide to the incredulous merchants, shouted, "Who wants to come across?"

One of the younger men quickly said he did. Christopher put him up on his broad shoulders and grabbed a bundle in each hand while the others, anxious, prayed to the Virgin Mary. He then proceeded to cross the river — and from the other side, the merchant, radiant, gestured enthusiastically to his companions and shouted that the giant was safe to use. Then, Christopher carried the remaining men over, followed by their packs. And, finally, he laid hold of the mules, frightened and braying, and conveyed them, and eventually the entire caravan, across to the other side, and all without letting a single animal's hide, a single pack rope, or a single man's shoe get wet. Having gathered together quietly off to one side, the men then placed in his palm a handful of money, they gave him a roll of rope, and they left him bread for a week.

Right away that same afternoon, Christopher, examining the harsh, wild place he was in, set about collecting some broken tree trunks and dry boughs and, jamming the bigger pieces of wood into the cracks and gaps in the rocks and running a rope from one point to another, was able to cobble together a kind of long, narrow lean-to shed under which his huge body could find shelter from the rain and snow. Later on, after having cleaned away the gravel from the roadway, he waited, seated in the great solitude of the place, for wayfarers to appear. Not long in arriving, over on the other bank, was a band of friars who, with their abbot mounted on a mule, were passing through. Christopher had scarcely seen them before he began crossing the river to get them — but the friars, terrified, were gesturing wildly at him that he not risk their lives in the waters of the wild river. But when they saw him arrive on their shore, enormous, with water pouring off him, and with his arms opened wide to receive them, they hesitated nevertheless, thinking him surely some sort of Devil's snare or deceit. The cross that the abbot drew through the air, and which act Christopher repeated on his own breast, quickly calmed them down, and they began to murmur among themselves that he must certainly be some sort of messenger from God sent to help them. One by one, and rolling up the hems of their habits, they rode Christopher across the river. In the middle of it, as they felt the waters furiously beating against the giant's waist, they cried out the name of the Virgin, the guiding star of shipwrecked sailors. Afterwards, when Christopher had deposited the friars on the other bank, safe and completely dry, they were amazed, and, rolling their habits back down and tying their sandals back on, they found themselves laughing at that huge, living bridge toiling away there in the waters. Christopher then brought the abbot over, and his mule, too. And the friars gave their blessings to the giant and his boxwood shelter.

There then began for Christopher a life of quiet and stability alongside the river. During the times when there were no travelers about, he would wait, seated on a large rock, and contemplate the running waters, or he would work away on extending the road, or, along one bank, at building, with stones, a type of quay, or jetty, where people could more easily climb up on his back. But most times, however, someone was always passing by, and — since Christopher was by now quite well known — the wayfarers, from way up on the hilltop, would come down shouting, "Hey, giant!" Others, more brutal, would — if Christopher was slow to respond — hurt and injure him. Still others, incited by the wine they'd consumed in the taverns along the way, would yank out his hair. But through it all, he, quiet and humble, would traverse the water for them. Occasionally, it was a knight who, with his heavy armor, would mash his shoulders and, laughing, prod him with his spurs. Other times it would be a great lady who, making a show of horror at Christopher's ugliness, would cover her face, and, once she was safely across on the other bank, would then flee from his strong hands and show her disgust. What took his greatest effort were the animals. There were flocks of sheep that could take him an entire day to get across. The warhorses, powerful and hard to control, would bite him on the arms. And the greyhounds, always barking, wanted to jump into the river — much to the displeasure of the noblemen, who would throw stones at him. But no effort was too great or too onerous for that good giant. He carried across the heaviest, hardest packs, the biggest barrels of wine, and enormous stones for the construction of the abbeys. He carried across bulls that were destined for some nobleman's herd. And he even carried across a band of lepers who were fleeing from a city and who left on his skin the pus of their fistulas.

If people did not pay him, he would lower his head and, with great humility, wish them well. If people did pay him, he would kiss the few copper coins they might give him — and then hide them under a stone so that he could later share this paltry recompense with beggars.

And thus did Christopher live for many long years. His head had become more and more bowed down with age and his great arms were not as powerful as they once had been. Sometimes, now, he would groan pitifully under the weight of heavy loads. All four of his limbs were like knotty tree trunks and swollen from the constant wetness. From all parts of him there issued the stench of slime and river scum. And his legs, always in the cold water, had taken on a greenish hue, as if they were the posts of a millrace.

Although his bed of dried tree branches was, for him, a place of sweet repose, whenever he heard voices calling for his help, it was these days with a groan that he lifted himself up from it. It now took him twice as long as it once did to pass back and forth against the river's powerful currents — and so the injuries he received became a constant source of suffering. To prop himself up in the rushing waters, as he sensed his strength diminishing, he'd had to fashion a sharp-pointed pole from a long piece of wood he'd found nearby. And with each and every winter now, as the river's water level and intensity would rise, he would wonder, in great distress, if he had sufficient strength left to overcome its furious currents yet again.

Nowadays, as soon as he had carried the wayfarers across and they continued on, Christopher would immediately lie down to rest. And he even found himself now begging of the travelers he helped that, out of a sense of charity, they leave him a little wine — even a little cordial wine to sustain him — to help him get through the hard nights. Oh, just a small amount would be fine, a mug full, nothing more.... If they did, he, Christopher, taking it cautiously and sparingly would make it last.

Then it came to pass that one night, in the deepest, darkest time of winter, when the wind was howling and it was cold and snowing and the river, running full and high, was roaring furiously, Christopher, now very old and hobbling and with open sores on his legs, was asleep in his bed, rendered wet from the elements, when, in the wild night, he heard a little voice cry out in great pain, from outside his hut, "Christopher! Christopher!"

With a groan, that good giant quickly stood up. And opening the flap of his hovel, he saw, in front of him, a little child, barefoot and standing on the grass with his hair flying about wildly in the wind and rain and clutching to his breast, with his little hands, the very white, very bright shirt that covered him. Taken aback, and with tears in his eyes, Christopher opened his arms and said, "Oh, my child! Who brought you here?"

And, shivering all over, in the cold and blowing snow, the little child murmured, "Christopher, Christopher, I'm all alone and lost, and because of who you are, I beg you to take me to my father's house!"

Christopher had already pulled from his own shoulders the hide he'd wrapped himself up in and covered the dear little body of the shivering boy with it. "Oh, my child," he then said. "Where is your father's house?"

The child extended his arm and pointed to the other shore, where the black mountains rose up steeply. And then he murmured, in a very low voice, "There, that distant place, and beyond . . . it's very far. . . ."

A fright then took hold of Christopher. Why, underneath the black goat skin, was the thin, white linen shirt of the child again shining so brightly in the black night? Very humbly, and bowing his head down to the boy, the good giant said, with an expression of great humility, "Oh, my child! Come, let me carry you in my arms."

The child raised his little arms up to him. Carefully and gently, Christopher lifted the boy up and placed him securely on his shoulders. But suddenly, under the immense weight that was crushing him, his knees buckled, striking a nearby rock. Oh, how heavy that boy was! With a great effort, Christopher steadied himself on his ancient, aching legs. Leaning heavily on his pole, Christopher headed down the path toward the raging river and plunged his feet into it. Immediately, he felt the powerful current roaring furiously all around him and throwing up foamy spume as far as the child's feet. Breathing hard, Christopher began to part the rushing water. The fierce wind was whistling and whipped his greying hair into his eyes, dulled, now, by time and the harsh conditions in which he lived. "Ah, my child, my child!," he said, as he struggled on. At each step, he felt the slimy riverbed under his feet slipping and sliding away from him. Leaning heavily on his pole for support, Christopher's entire body was trembling. And the cold water, whipped into a white foam, tore at him furiously with a fearful surging. In the dense darkness, he could distinguish nothing; he could not even tell where the other shore was. Thick, heavy hailstones began to crash down upon him, and the child, shivering with cold, clung to him and snuggled against his face. Now, the fearful waters had reached up as far as Christopher's chest. He stumbled against a rock and, when he'd regained his balance, he felt the furious, freezing waters splashing up against the hairs of his beard. Christopher threw aside his staff and, with both hands, raised the child high into the air. But he could barely hold him aloft like that, and large waves began to strike him in the face. Gasping now, and trying to get his head free from the pounding water so he could breathe, Christopher stopped for a moment to recover and he was forced to drink in the salty spume. Heavy wooden beams swept along by the powerful current crashed against his body and battered it. His feet were being ripped and torn by the sharp rocks. And yet, through it all, Christopher, making an enormous effort, with his arms still extended upward, and shaking all over, held on, keeping the child up high and safe. And, with groans now louder than the howls of the wind, he thrust his great chest forward and pushed on. Twice his knees grew weak and were about to buckle and throw him and the child under the raging torrent; twice, and with superhuman efforts, he steadied himself, all the while holding the child up on high. The waters had now reached the level of his beard, and the foam kicked up by the waves wet his eyes and face. Panting hard, and with his hands trembling under the tremendous weight of the child, Christopher felt his strength ebbing away. But then his feet found a firm rock, and the water began to recede, going down once again to his chest. Though offering solid footing, the rock was nevertheless slippery, and so his steps, each one a struggle, were far from steady or sure. And it was truly only an effort springing from the innermost part of his soul that allowed Christopher, still struggling for each and every breath, to steady himself and keep going. But, finally, they were emerging from the river. The water was now only at his waist. And the roar of the current here seemed softer and more remote. Huge stones were appearing from beneath the water's surface. Finally, only Christopher's feet, which only now did he realize were lacerated, remained under the water. With one more mighty effort, he pulled himself out of the river and was safely on the other bank, still clasping the child tightly against his breast.

But with that supreme effort, Christopher's great strength was spent. He could do no more. And so he was sitting down, exhausted, on a rock, when the child, in a hushed voice, told him that he was not to stop, that he was to go on, and that he was to take him to his father's house. And so Christopher, still laboring for every breath, began to climb the steep path that led up into the mountains the child had pointed toward. A vague brightness seemed to flicker in the far-off sky beyond them. And the rocks and fir trees emerged from the dense darkness that enveloped them. A chill seemed to pass through the air — and Christopher was shivering in his coarse woolen coat, still wet from the river and dripping on the soft ground. And, in a low voice, he murmured, "Ah, my child! My child . . . !"

Steeper and steeper and winding in between rocks and boulders, the path led ever upward into the mountains. And Christopher, completely bent over now, his hair falling down over his face, and sweating profusely, was gasping for air with every step. Would he never get to the boy's dwelling place? At that very moment, Christopher felt a terrible pain in his heart! It was the terror of failing, of falling to the ground, bereft of strength and lifeless, and of the child being left there, in that brutal wilderness, alone and at the mercy of the wild animals and exposed to the storms. At every step, now, Christopher, weakening fast and growing faint, had to put his hand on a rock or grab hold of a fir tree branch to keep himself upright. And the brightness seemed to grow . . . at the top of the mountain, he thought he could see the pale white glow of the snow. "Oh, my child," Christopher said, "where is your father's house?"

"Further, Christopher, much further. . . ."

And that good giant, wrapping up the boy's feet in the folds of the goatskin that the wind had undone, struggled on, uttering long, low groans along the unending path, which grew narrower and narrower, winding its way between rocky formations rising up from out of enormous brambles. Finally, Christopher could hardly take another step. The sharp edges of the rocks cut and bruised his arms and the long spines of the bushes, sticking out in all directions, tore at the rough skin of his face. And yet he went on! His wounds were now dripping blood and his eyes were growing so dim that he could scarcely make out the path, which seemed to sway from side to side, as if loosened by an earthly tremor. In the meantime, a light, brighter now and rose colored, had suddenly arisen from behind the line of craggy mounts up ahead.

But, unable to give any more, Christopher had come to a halt. With the child clutched in his arms, he remained there, leaning up against a great stone, gasping for breath.

"Where is your father's house?," he said. "Further, Christopher, further still...."

Making a truly prodigious effort, our good giant then pressed on, virtually collapsing at each step of the way, his eyes growing darker and darker, thrusting his hand out in quest of something to help prop himself up, and with thick drops of sweat now mixing with thick drops of blood, stumbling ever forward and higher, onward, ever onward, toward the final summit. In the utter and total exhaustion that had overtaken them, Christopher's feet were moving randomly now, as if of their own volition. A great coldness invaded his arms and legs and then his entire body. He suddenly felt as weak as the child he bore on his shoulders. And, at the summit of the mountain, he finally stopped, his great strength totally spent. It was the end. A great new morning sun was being born, and it bathed the entire earth in its light. Christopher placed the child on the ground and then collapsed at his side, holding out his arms one final time. He was dying. But when he felt his thick, powerful hands touch those of the child, the earth beneath his feet seemed to fall away from him. Christopher then opened his eyes and, in a moment of incomparable splendor, he recognized Jesus Christ, our Lord and Savior, as small as when he'd been born in the manger and who now, sweetly, kindly, and through the clear, bright morning light, was bearing him up to Heaven.

Adamastor Series

SERIES EDITOR / ANNA M. KLOBUCKA

Chaos and Splendor & Other Essays
EDUARDO LOURENÇO
EDITED BY CARLOS VELOSO

Producing Presences: Branching Out from Gumbrecht's Work
EDITED BY VICTOR K. MENDES
AND JOÃO CEZAR DE CASTRO
ROCHA

Sonnets and Other Poems
LUÍS DE CAMÕES / TRANSLATED
BY RICHARD ZENITH

The Traveling Eye: Retrospection, Vision, and Prophecy in the Portuguese Renaissance
FERNANDO GIL AND HELDER
MACEDO / TRANSLATED BY
K. DAVID JACKSON, ANNA M.
KLOBUCKA, KENNETH
KRABBENHOFT, RICHARD ZENITH

The Sermon of Saint Anthony to the Fish and Other Texts
ANTÓNIO VIEIRA / TRANSLATED
BY GREGORY RABASSA

The Correspondence of Fradique Mendes: A Novel
JOSÉ DE MARIA DE EÇA DE
QUEIRÓS / TRANSLATED BY
GREGORY RABASSA

The Relic: A Novel
JOSÉ DE MARIA DE EÇA DE
QUEIRÓS / PREFACE BY HAROLD
BLOOM / TRANSLATED BY
AUBREY F. G. BELL

Maiden and Modest: A Renaissance Pastoral Romance
BERNARDIM RIBEIRO
FOREWORD BY EARL E. FITZ
TRANSLATED BY GREGORY
RABASSA

Saint Christopher: A Novella
JOSÉ DE MARIA DE EÇA DE
QUEIRÓS / FOREWORD BY CARLOS
REIS / TRANSLATED BY GREGORY
RABASSA AND EARL E. FITZ